GENOCIDE & PERSECUTION

| Indonesia

Titles in the Genocide and Persecution Series

GENOCIDE & PERSECUTION

I Indonesia

Noah Berlatsky
Book Editor

Frank Chalk
Consulting Editor

GREENHAVEN PRESS
A part of Gale, Cengage Learning

GALE
CENGAGE Learning·

Farmington Hills, Mich • San Francisco • New York • Waterville, Maine
Meriden, Conn • Mason, Ohio • Chicago

Elizabeth Des Chenes, *Director, Content Strategy*
Cynthia Sanner, *Publisher*
Douglas Dentino, *Manager, New Product*

For more information, contact:
Greenhaven Press
27500 Drake Rd.
Farmington Hills, MI 48331-3535
Or you can visit our Internet site at gale.cengage.com.

For product information and technology assistance, contact us at:

Gale Customer Support, 1-800-877-4253
For permission to use material from this text or product, submit all requests online at
www.cengage.com/permissions

Further permissions questions can be emailed to permissionrequest@cengage.com

Every effort is made to ensure that Greenhaven Press accurately reflects the original intent of the authors. Every effort has been made to trace the owners of copyrighted material.

Cover image © Bettmann/Corbis.
Interior barbed wire artwork © f9photos, used under license from Shutterstock.com.

LIBRARY OF CONGRESS CATALOGING-IN-PUBLICATION DATA

Indonesia (Greenhaven Press)
   Indonesia / Noah Berlatsky, book editor.
     pages cm -- (Genocide and persecution)
   Includes bibliographical references and index.
   ISBN 978-0-7377-6898-5 (hardcover)
  1. Indonesia--History--Coup d'état, 1965--Sources. 2. Indonesia--Politics and government--1950-1966--Sources. 3. Partai Komunis Indonesia. 4. Political atrocities--Indonesia. I. Berlatsky, Noah, editor of compilation. II. Cribb, R. B. Overview of the 1965 killings in Indonesia. Contains (work): III. Title. IV. Series: Genocide and persecution.
   DS644.32.I53 2014
   959.803'5--dc23
                                   2013044342

Printed in the United States of America
1 2 3 4 5 6 7 18 17 16 15 14

Contents

Chapter 1: Historical Background on the Indonesian Genocide of 1965

Chapter 2: Controversies Surrounding the Indonesian Genocide of 1965

An Australian historian argues that ethnic and political identities over-lapped in Indonesia to such an extent that the 1965 anti-Communist killings could be considered genocide.

Chapter 3: Personal Narratives

Preface

> *"For the dead and the living, we must*
> *bear witness."*
>
> *Elie Wiesel, Nobel laureate and*
> *Holocaust survivor*

The histories of many nations are shaped by horrific events involving torture, violent repression, and systematic mass killings. The inhumanity of such events is difficult to comprehend, yet understanding why such events take place, what impact they have on society, and how they may be prevented in the future is vitally important. The Genocide and Persecution series provides readers with anthologies of previously published materials on acts of genocide, crimes against humanity, and other instances of extreme persecution, with an emphasis on events taking place in the twentieth and twenty-first centuries. The series offers essential historical background on these significant events in modern world history, presents the issues and controversies surrounding the events, and provides first-person narratives from people whose lives were altered by the events. By providing primary sources, as well as analysis of crucial issues, these volumes help develop critical-thinking skills and support global connections. In addition, the series directly addresses curriculum standards focused on informational text and literary nonfiction and explicitly promotes literacy in history and social studies.

Each Genocide and Persecution volume focuses on genocide, crimes against humanity, or severe persecution. Material from a variety of primary and secondary sources presents a multinational perspective on the event. Articles are carefully edited and introduced to provide context for readers. The series includes volumes on significant and widely studied events like the Holocaust, as well as events that are less often studied, such as the East Pakistan genocide in what is now Bangladesh. Some volumes focus on multiple events endured by a specific people, such as the Kurds, or multiple events enacted over time by a particular oppressor or in a particular location, such as the People's Republic of China.

Each volume is organized into three chapters. The first chapter provides readers with general background information and uses primary sources such as testimony from tribunals or international courts, documents or speeches from world leaders, and legislative text. The second chapter presents multinational perspectives on issues and controversies and addresses current implications or long-lasting effects of the event. Viewpoints explore such topics as root causes; outside interventions, if any; the impact on the targeted group and the region; and the contentious issues that arose in the aftermath. The third chapter presents first-person narratives from affected people, including survivors, family members of victims, perpetrators, officials, aid workers, and other witnesses.

In addition, numerous features are included in each volume of Genocide and Persecution:

- An annotated **table of contents** provides a brief summary of each essay in the volume.
- A **foreword** gives important background information on the recognition, definition, and study of genocide in recent history and examines current efforts focused on the prevention of future atrocities.
- A **chronology** offers important dates leading up to, during, and following the event.
- **Primary sources**—including historical newspaper accounts, testimony, and personal narratives—are among the varied selections in the anthology.
- **Illustrations**—including a world map, photographs, charts, graphs, statistics, and tables—are closely tied

to the text and chosen to help readers understand key points or concepts.

- **Sidebars**—including biographies of key figures and overviews of earlier or related historical events—offer additional content.
- **Pedagogical features**—including analytical exercises, writing prompts, and group activities—introduce each chapter and help reinforce the material. These features promote proficiency in writing, speaking, and listening skills and literacy in history and social studies.
- A **glossary** defines key terms, as needed.
- An annotated list of international **organizations to contact** presents sources of additional information on the volume topic.
- A **list of primary source documents** provides an annotated list of reports, treaties, resolutions, and judicial decisions related to the volume topic.
- A **for further research** section offers a bibliography of books, periodical articles, and Internet sources and an annotated section of other items such as films and websites.
- A comprehensive subject **index** provides access to key people, places, events, and subjects cited in the text.

The Genocide and Persecution series illuminates atrocities that cannot and should not be forgotten. By delving deeply into these events from a variety of perspectives, students and other readers are provided with the information they need to think critically about the past and its implications for the future.

Foreword

The term *genocide* often appears in news stories and other literature. It is not widely known, however, that the core meaning of the term comes from a legal definition, and the concept became part of international criminal law only in 1951 when the United Nations Convention on the Prevention and Punishment of the Crime of Genocide came into force. The word *genocide* appeared in print for the first time in 1944 when Raphael Lemkin, a Polish Jewish refugee from Adolf Hitler's World War II invasion of Eastern Europe, invented the term and explored its meaning in his pioneering book *Axis Rule in Occupied Europe*.

Humanity's Recognition of Genocide and Persecution

Lemkin understood that throughout the history of the human race there have always been leaders who thought they could solve their problems not only through victory in war, but also by destroying entire national, ethnic, racial, or religious groups. Such annihilations of entire groups, in Lemkin's view, deprive the world of the very cultural diversity and richness in languages, traditions, values, and practices that distinguish the human race from all other life on earth. Genocide is not only unjust, it threatens the very existence and progress of human civilization, in Lemkin's eyes.

Looking to the past, Lemkin understood that the prevailing coarseness and brutality of earlier human societies and the lower value placed on human life obscured the existence of genocide. Sacrifice and exploitation, as well as torture and public execution, had been common at different times in history. Looking toward a more humane future, Lemkin asserted the need to punish—and when possible prevent—a crime for which there had been no name until he invented it.

Legal Definitions of Genocide

On December 9, 1948, the United Nations adopted its Convention on the Prevention and Punishment of the Crime of Genocide (UNGC). Under Article II, genocide

> means any of the following acts committed with intent to destroy, in whole or in part, a national, ethnical, racial or religious group, as such:
>
> (a) Killing members of the group;
>
> (b) Causing serious bodily or mental harm to members of the group;
>
> (c) Deliberately inflicting on the group conditions of life calculated to bring about its physical destruction in whole or in part;
>
> (d) Imposing measures intended to prevent births within the group;
>
> (e) Forcibly transferring children of the group to another group.

Article III of the convention defines the elements of the crime of genocide, making punishable:

> (a) Genocide;
>
> (b) Conspiracy to commit genocide;
>
> (c) Direct and public incitement to commit genocide;
>
> (d) Attempt to commit genocide;
>
> (e) Complicity in genocide.

After intense debate, the architects of the convention excluded acts committed with intent to destroy social, political, and economic groups from the definition of genocide. Thus, attempts to destroy whole social classes—the physically and mentally challenged, and homosexuals, for example—are not acts of genocide under the terms of the UNGC. These groups achieved a belated but very significant measure of protection under international criminal law in the Rome Statute of the International Criminal

Court, adopted at a conference on July 17, 1998, and entered into force on July 1, 2002.

The Rome Statute defined a crime against humanity in the following way:

> any of the following acts when committed as part of a widespread and systematic attack directed against any civilian population:
>
> (a) Murder;
>
> (b) Extermination;
>
> (c) Enslavement;
>
> (d) Deportation or forcible transfer of population;
>
> (e) Imprisonment or other severe deprivation of physical liberty in violation of fundamental rules of international law;
>
> (f) Torture;
>
> (g) Rape, sexual slavery, enforced prostitution, forced pregnancy, enforced sterilization, or any other form of sexual violence of comparable gravity;
>
> (h) Persecution against any identifiable group or collectivity on political, racial, national, ethnic, cultural, religious, gender . . . or other grounds that are universally recognized as impermissible under international law, in connection with any act referred to in this paragraph or any crime within the jurisdiction of this Court;
>
> (i) Enforced disappearance of persons;
>
> (j) The crime of apartheid;
>
> (k) Other inhumane acts of a similar character intentionally causing great suffering, or serious injury to body or to mental or physical health.

Although genocide is often ranked as "the crime of crimes," in practice prosecutors find it much easier to convict perpetrators of crimes against humanity rather than genocide under domestic laws. However, while Article I of the UNGC declares that countries adhering to the UNGC recognize genocide as "a crime under international law which they undertake to prevent and to punish," the Rome Statute provides no comparable international mechanism for the prosecution of crimes against humanity. A treaty would help individual countries and international institutions introduce measures to prevent crimes against humanity, as well as open more avenues to the domestic and international prosecution of war criminals.

The Evolving Laws of Genocide

In the aftermath of the serious crimes committed against civilians in the former Yugoslavia since 1991 and the Rwanda genocide of 1994, the United Nations Security Council created special international courts to bring the alleged perpetrators of these events to justice. While the UNGC stands as the standard definition of genocide in law, the new courts contributed significantly to today's nuanced meaning of genocide, crimes against humanity, ethnic cleansing, and serious war crimes in international criminal law.

Also helping to shape contemporary interpretations of such mass atrocity crimes are the special and mixed courts for Sierra Leone, Cambodia, Lebanon, and Iraq, which may be the last of their type in light of the creation of the International Criminal Court (ICC), with its broad jurisdiction over mass atrocity crimes in all countries that adhere to the Rome Statute of the ICC. The Yugoslavia and Rwanda tribunals have already clarified the law of genocide, ruling that rape can be prosecuted as a weapon in committing genocide, evidence of intent can be absent when convicting low-level perpetrators of genocide, and public incitement to commit genocide is a crime even if genocide does not immediately follow the incitement.

Several current controversies about genocide are worth noting and will require more research in the future:

1. Dictators accused of committing genocide or persecution may hold onto power more tightly for fear of becoming

vulnerable to prosecution after they step down. Therefore, do threats of international indictments of these alleged perpetrators actually delay transfers of power to more representative rulers, thereby causing needless suffering?

2. Would the large sum of money spent for international retributive justice be better spent on projects directly benefiting the survivors of genocide and persecution?

3. Can international courts render justice impartially or do they deliver only "victors' justice," that is the application of one set of rules to judge the vanquished and a different and laxer set of rules to judge the victors?

It is important to recognize that the law of genocide is constantly evolving, and scholars searching for the roots and early warning signs of genocide may prefer to use their own definitions of genocide in their work. While the UNGC stands as the standard definition of genocide in law, the debate over its interpretation and application will never end. The ultimate measure of the value of any definition of genocide is its utility for identifying the roots of genocide and preventing future genocides.

Motives for Genocide and Early Warning Signs

When identifying past cases of genocide, many scholars work with some version of the typology of motives published in 1990 by historian Frank Chalk and sociologist Kurt Jonassohn in their book *The History and Sociology of Genocide*. The authors identify the following four motives and acknowledge that they may overlap, or several lesser motives might also drive a perpetrator:

1. To eliminate a real or potential threat, as in Imperial Rome's decision to annihilate Carthage in 146 B.C.

2. To spread terror among real or potential enemies, as in Genghis Khan's destruction of city-states and people who rebelled against the Mongols in the thirteenth century.

3. To acquire economic wealth, as in the case of the Massachusetts Puritans' annihilation of the native Pequot people in 1637.
4. To implement a belief, theory, or an ideology, as in the case of Germany's decision under Hitler and the Nazis to destroy completely the Jewish people of Europe from 1941 to 1945.

Although these motives represent differing goals, they share common early warning signs of genocide. A good example of genocide in recent times that could have been prevented through close attention to early warning signs was the genocide of 1994 inflicted on the people labeled as "Tutsi" in Rwanda. Between 1959 and 1963, the predominantly Hutu political parties in power stigmatized all Tutsi as members of a hostile racial group, violently forcing their leaders and many civilians into exile in neighboring countries through a series of assassinations and massacres. Despite systematic exclusion of Tutsi from service in the military, government security agencies, and public service, as well as systematic discrimination against them in higher education, hundreds of thousands of Tutsi did remain behind in Rwanda. Government-issued cards identified each Rwandan as Hutu or Tutsi.

A generation later, some Tutsi raised in refugee camps in Uganda and elsewhere joined together, first organizing politically and then militarily, to reclaim a place in their homeland. When the predominantly Tutsi Rwanda Patriotic Front invaded Rwanda from Uganda in October 1990, extremist Hutu political parties demonized all of Rwanda's Tutsi as traitors, ratcheting up hate propaganda through radio broadcasts on government-run Radio Rwanda and privately owned radio station RTLM. Within the print media, *Kangura* and other publications used vicious cartoons to further demonize Tutsi and to stigmatize any Hutu who dared advocate bringing Tutsi into the government. Massacres of dozens and later hundreds of Tutsi sprang up even as Rwandans prepared to elect a coalition government led by moderate political parties, and as the United Nations dispatched a small international military force led by Canadian general Roméo Dallaire to oversee the elections and political transition. Late in 1992, an international human rights organization's investigating team detected the hate propaganda campaign, verified systematic massacres of Tutsi, and warned the international community that Rwanda had already entered the early stages of genocide, to no avail. On April 6, 1994, Rwanda's genocidal killing accelerated at an alarming pace when someone shot down the airplane flying Rwandan president Juvenal Habyarimana home from peace talks in Arusha, Tanzania.

Hundreds of thousands of Tutsi civilians—including children, women, and the elderly—died horrible deaths because the world ignored the early warning signs of the genocide and refused to act. Prominent among those early warning signs were: 1) systematic, government-decreed discrimination against the Tutsi as members of a supposed racial group; 2) government-issued identity cards labeling every Tutsi as a member of a racial group; 3) hate propaganda casting all Tutsi as subversives and traitors; 4) organized assassinations and massacres targeting Tutsi; and 5) indoctrination of militias and special military units to believe that all Tutsi posed a genocidal threat to the existence of Hutu and would enslave Hutu if they ever again became the rulers of Rwanda.

Genocide Prevention and the Responsibility to Protect

The shock waves emanating from the Rwanda genocide forced world leaders at least to acknowledge in principle that the national sovereignty of offending nations cannot trump the responsibility of those governments to prevent the infliction of mass atrocities on their own people. When governments violate that obligation, the member states of the United Nations have a responsibility to get involved. Such involvement can take the form of, first, offering to help the local government change its ways through technical advice and development aid, and second—if the local government persists in assaulting its own people— initiating armed intervention to protect the civilians at risk. In 2005 the United Nations began to implement the Responsibility to Protect initiative, a framework of principles to guide the international community in preventing mass atrocities.

As in many real-world domains, theory and practice often diverge. Genocide and crimes against humanity are rooted in problems that produce failing states: poverty, poor education, extreme nationalism, lawlessness, dictatorship, and corruption. Implementing the principles of the Responsibility to Protect doctrine burdens intervening state leaders with the necessity of addressing each of those problems over a long period of time. And when those problems prove too intractable and complex to solve easily, the citizens of the intervening nations may lose patience, voting out the leader who initiated the intervention. Arguments based solely on humanitarian principles fail to overcome such concerns. What is needed to persuade political leaders to stop preventable mass atrocities are compelling arguments based on their own national interests.

Preventable mass atrocities threaten the national interests of all states in five specific ways:

1. Mass atrocities create conditions that engender widespread and concrete threats from terrorism, piracy, and other forms of lawlessness on the land and sea;

2. Mass atrocities facilitate the spread of warlordism, whose tentacles block affordable access to vital raw materials produced in the affected country and threaten the prosperity of all nations that depend on the consumption of these resources;

3. Mass atrocities trigger cascades of refugees and internally displaced populations that, combined with climate change and growing international air travel, will accelerate the worldwide incidence of lethal infectious diseases;

4. Mass atrocities spawn single-interest parties and political agendas that drown out more diverse political discourse in the countries where the atrocities take place and in the countries that host large numbers of refugees. Xenophobia and nationalist backlashes are the predictable consequences of government indifference to mass atrocities elsewhere that could have been prevented through early actions;

5. Mass atrocities foster the spread of national and transnational criminal networks trafficking in drugs, women, arms, contraband, and laundered money.

Alerting elected political representatives to the consequences of mass atrocities should be part of every student movement's agenda in the twenty-first century. Adam Smith, the great political economist and author of *The Wealth of Nations*, put it best when he wrote: "It is not from the benevolence of the butcher, the brewer, or the baker that we expect our dinner, but from their regard to their own interest." Self-interest is a powerful engine for good in the marketplace and can be an equally powerful motive and source of inspiration for state action to prevent genocide and mass persecution. In today's new global village, the lives we save may be our own.

Frank Chalk

Frank Chalk, who has a doctorate from the University of Wisconsin-Madison, is a professor of history and director of the Montreal Institute for Genocide and Human Rights Studies at Concordia University in Montreal, Canada. He is coauthor, with Kurt Jonassohn, of The History and Sociology of Genocide *(1990); coauthor with General Roméo Dallaire, Kyle Matthews, Carla Barqueiro, and Simon Doyle of* Mobilizing the Will to Intervene: Leadership to Prevent Mass Atrocities *(2010); and associate editor of the three-volume Macmillan Reference USA* Encyclopedia of Genocide and Crimes Against Humanity *(2004). Chalk served as president of the International Association of Genocide Scholars from June 1999 to June 2001. His current research focuses on the use of radio and television broadcasting in the incitement and prevention of genocide, and domestic laws on genocide. For more information on genocide and examples of the experiences of people displaced by genocide and other human rights violations, interested readers can consult the websites of the Montreal Institute for Genocide and Human Rights Studies (http://migs.concordia.ca) and the Montreal Life Stories project (www.lifestoriesmontreal.ca).*

World Map

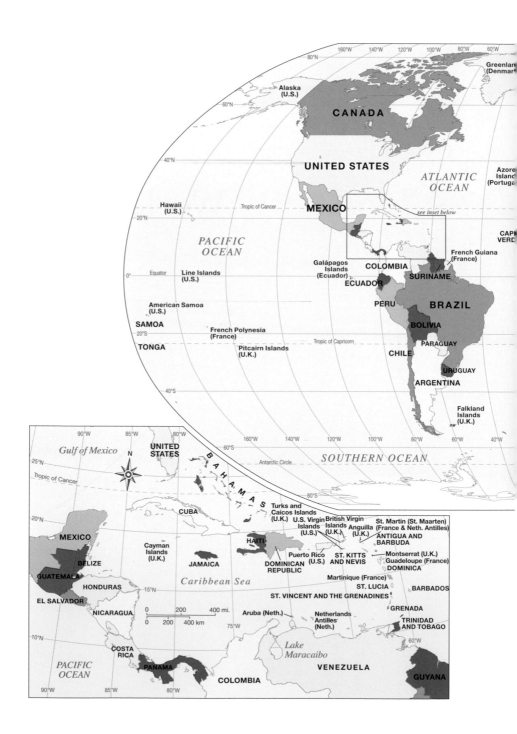

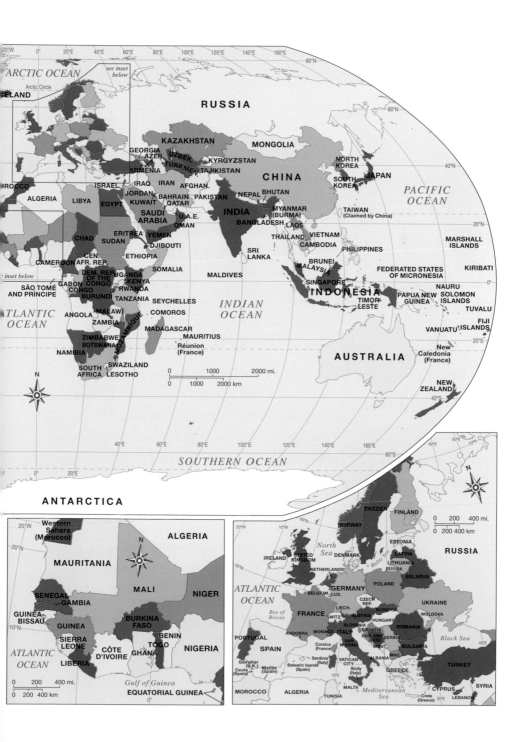

ARCTIC OCEAN

Arctic Circle

ICELAND

RUSSIA

KAZAKHSTAN

MONGOLIA

GEORGIA
AZER.
UZBEK.
TURKMEN.
KYRGYZSTAN
ARMENIA
TAJIKISTAN

NORTH
KOREA

JAPAN

MOROCCO

ISRAEL
IRAQ
IRAN
AFGHAN.
CHINA
SOUTH
KOREA

PACIFIC
OCEAN

ALGERIA
LIBYA
EGYPT
JORDAN
KUWAIT
BAHRAIN
QATAR
PAKISTAN
NEPAL
BHUTAN

SAUDI
ARABIA
U.A.E.
OMAN
INDIA
MYANMAR
(BURMA)
BANGLADESH
LAOS

TAIWAN
(Claimed by China)

CHAD
SUDAN
ERITREA
YEMEN
DJIBOUTI
THAILAND
VIETNAM
CAMBODIA

MARSHALL
ISLANDS

CEN.
AFR. REP.
ETHIOPIA
SRI
LANKA
PHILIPPINES

CAMEROON
BRUNEI
MALAYSIA

inset below
DEM. REP.
OF THE
CONGO
UGANDA
SOMALIA
MALDIVES
SINGAPORE
INDONESIA

FEDERATED STATES
OF MICRONESIA

KIRIBATI

SÃO TOMÉ
AND PRÍNCIPE
GABON
CONGO
KENYA
RWANDA
NAURU

ATLANTIC
OCEAN
BURUNDI
TANZANIA
SEYCHELLES
INDIAN
OCEAN
TIMOR-
LESTE
PAPUA NEW
GUINEA
SOLOMON
ISLANDS

ANGOLA
MALAWI
COMOROS
TUVALU

ZAMBIA
FIJI
VANUATU
ISLANDS

ZIMBABWE
MOZAMBIQUE
MADAGASCAR
MAURITIUS

NAMIBIA
BOTSWANA
Réunion
(France)

AUSTRALIA
New
Caledonia
(France)

SOUTH
AFRICA
SWAZILAND
LESOTHO

0   1000   2000 mi.
0   1000   2000 km

NEW
ZEALAND

SOUTHERN OCEAN

ANTARCTICA

Western
Sahara
(Morocco)

ALGERIA

SWEDEN
FINLAND

NORWAY

ESTONIA

MAURITANIA

MALI

NIGER

IRELAND
UNITED
KINGDOM
North
Sea
DENMARK

LATVIA
LITHUANIA
RUSSIA

RUSSIA

SENEGAL
GAMBIA

NETHERLANDS

BELARUS

GUINEA-
BISSAU
GUINEA

BURKINA
FASO
BENIN

ATLANTIC
OCEAN
GERMANY
BELGIUM
LUX.
POLAND

UKRAINE

CZECH
REP.
LIECH.

SIERRA
LEONE
CÔTE
D'IVOIRE
TOGO
GHANA
NIGERIA

Bay of
Biscay
FRANCE
SWITZ.
AUSTRIA
SLOVAKIA
HUNGARY
MOLDOVA

ROMANIA

LIBERIA

ATLANTIC
OCEAN
Gulf of Guinea
EQUATORIAL GUINEA

PORTUGAL
ANDORRA
MONACO
SLOVENIA
CROATIA
ITALY
SAN
MARINO
BOS. AND
HERZ.
SERBIA
BULGARIA

Black Sea

0   200   400 mi.
0   200 400 km

SPAIN
Corsica
(France)
Sardinia
(Italy)
MONT.
MAC.
ALBANIA
GREECE
TURKEY

Gibraltar
(U.K.)
Ceuta
(Spain)
Melilla
(Spain)
Balearic Island
(Spain)
VATICAN
CITY
Sicily
(Italy)

CYPRUS
SYRIA

MOROCCO
ALGERIA
TUNISIA
MALTA
Crete
(Greece)
Mediterranean
Sea
LEBANON

0   200   400 mi.
0   200 400 km

see inset
below

inset below

17 |

Chronology

Early 1900s	The Dutch complete the process, begun in the 1600s, of unifying Indonesia under their rule.
1927	Political leader Sukarno establishes a party to fight for Indonesia's independence.
1930	After his arrest by colonial authorities, Sukarno makes a series of famous speeches at his trial. He is still sentenced to a year in prison.
1934	Sukarno is arrested again and exiled to a distant part of Indonesia.
1942	During World War II, Japan invades Indonesia. Since both oppose the Dutch colonial government, the Japanese form ties with Sukarno, helping him return from exile.
1945	The Japanese are defeated at the end of World War II. Sukarno declares Indonesian independence under his government, and a guerrilla war against remaining Dutch forces begins.
1949	The Dutch give up their attempt to regain their colony and recognize Indonesian independence.
Early 1950s	Indonesia's domestic politics are fragmented and contentious, though Sukarno retains control.

1956–1957	Regional military commanders rebel against Sukarno. They receive aid from the American CIA.
December 1957	Sukarno takes government control of more than 200 Dutch companies that had dominated the economy.
1958	Sukarno's government defeats the rebel military commanders.
1963	Sukarno is named president for life. His rule becomes increasingly authoritarian, and his regime grows closer to Communist Russia and China and is supported by the Indonesian Communist party, or PKI.
October 1, 1965	Six senior Indonesian army generals are kidnapped and killed by a group called the September 30 Movement. The movement attempts to take over the Indonesian government in a coup.
1965–1966	The military accuses the PKI, the Indonesian Communist Party, of orchestrating the coup. The PKI denies the charge, but this does not stop the murder of hundreds of thousands of accused Communists.
March 1967	Weakened by the destruction of his allies in the Communist Party, Sukarno is forced to transfer power to Suharto, general of the Indonesian army.
1967–1968	Suharto establishes the New Order, which increases the power of the

	military at all levels of Indonesian society. Suharto is effectively the dictator of Indonesia.
1976	Indonesia invades and conquers the island of East Timor.
1997–1998	The Indonesian economic crisis leads to the fall of Suharto's government after thirty-one years.
1999	East Timor declares independence, leading to rampant violence by pro-Indonesia militias. East Timor is placed under UN administration as a means of stopping the violence.
2002	East Timor gains independence.
2004	A massive tidal wave kills more than 220,000 people in Indonesia.
2008	Former president Suharto dies.

CHAPTER 1

Historical Background on the Indonesian Genocide of 1965

Chapter Exercises

STATISTICS

	Indonesia
Total Area	1,904,569 square kilometers World ranking: 15
Population	251,160,124 (July 2013 est.) World ranking: 4
Ethnic Groups	Javanese 40.6%, Sundanese 15%, Madurese 3.3%, Minangkabau 2.7%, Betawi 2.4%, Bugis 2.4%, Bantenese 2%, Banjarese 1.7%, other or unspecified 29.9% (2000 census)
Religions	Muslim 86.1%, Protestant 5.7%, Roman Catholic 3%, Hindu 1.8%, other or unspecified 3.4% (2000 census)
Literacy (total population)	90.4%
GDP	$1,237 trillion (2012 est.) World ranking: 16

Source: *The World Factbook*. Washington, DC: Central Intelligence Agency, 2013. www.cia.gov.

1. Analyzing Statistics

Question 1: Does any ethnic group in Indonesia comprise a majority of the population? Do the statistics about ethnic groups give you information about who was targeted in the 1965 genocide? Explain your answer.

Question 2: Which is the largest religious group in Indonesia? Did this group play a significant role in the genocide? Were other religious groups targeted? Explain your answer.

Question 3: What rank is Indonesia in population? What rank is it in total area? Does this mean that Indonesia is crowded or sparsely populated? What effect might this population density have had on the killings in 1965?

2. Writing Prompt

Write an article describing an anti-Communist purge in an Indonesian village. Begin the article with a strong title that will captivate the audience. Include any appropriate background that will help readers better understand the event. Give details that explain the event and address the questions of who, what, when, where, and why.

3. Group Activity

In small groups, discuss the Suharto administration's involvement in genocide. Give a speech making a recommendation as to what the international community should have done with regard to Suharto following the killings.

Overview of the 1965 Killings in Indonesia

Robert Cribb

Robert Cribb is a professor of history at the Australian National University. In the following viewpoint, he provides an overview of the Indonesian genocide of 1965. He explains that the genocide began after a coup attempt that seemed linked to the PKI, the Indonesian Communist Party. Conservative generals cleverly exploited those links and used the resulting fear of communism to orchestrate the fall of President Sukarno and a wave of mass killings. Cribb says that five hundred thousand to 3 million people died. Many more were detained, and prejudice against the families of those killed or detained continued officially into the 2000s. Even now, Indonesia has not fully repudiated the killings, Cribb says, and as a result many details of the violence remain unknown.

During about five months, from late October 1965 until March 1966, approximately half a million members of the Indonesian Communist Party (Partai Komunis Indonesia, PKI) were killed by army units and anticommunist militias. At the time of its destruction, the PKI was the largest communist party in the non-communist world and was a major contender for power in

Robert Cribb, "Indonesia," as in *Encyclopedia of Genocide and Crimes Against Humanity*, ed. Dinah L. Shelton, volume two. MacMillan Reference: 2005, pp. 516–521. From *Encyclopedia of Genocide and Crimes Against Humanity*, first edition. © 2005 Cengage/Nelson.

Indonesia. President Sukarno's Guided Democracy had maintained an uneasy balance between the PKI and its leftist allies on one hand and a conservative coalition of military, religious, and liberal groups, presided over by Sukarno, on the other. Sukarno was a spellbinding orator and an accomplished ideologist, having woven the Indonesia's principal rival ideologies into an eclectic formula called NASAKOM (nationalism, religion, communism), but he was ailing, and there was a widespread feeling that either the communists or their opponents would soon seize power.

September 30

The catalyst for the killings was a coup in Jakarta, undertaken by the September 30 Movement, but actually carried out on October 1, 1965. Although many aspects of the coup remain uncertain, it appears to have been the work of junior army officers and a special bureau of the PKI answering to the party chairman, D.N. Aidit. The aim of the coup was to forestall a predicted military coup, planned for Armed Forces Day (October 5), by kidnapping the senior generals believed to be the rival coup plotters. After some of the generals were killed in botched kidnapping attempts, however, and after Sukarno refused to support the September 30 Movement, its leaders went further than previously planned and attempted to seize power. They were unprepared for such a drastic action, however, and the takeover attempt was defeated within twenty-four hours by the senior surviving general, Suharto, who was commander of the Army's Strategic Reserve, KOSTRAD.

There was no clear proof at the time that the coup had been the work of the PKI. Party involvement was suggested by the presence of Aidit at the plotters' headquarters in Halim Airforce Base, just south of Jakarta, and by the involvement of members of the communist-affiliated People's Youth (Pemuda Rakyat) in some of the operations, but the public pronouncements and activities of the September 30 Movement gave it the appearance of being an internal army movement. Nonetheless, for many observers it seemed likely that the party was behind the coup.

The PKI

Partai Komunis Indonesia (PKI), or the Indonesian Communist Party. The PKI was founded in May 1920 to succeed the Indies Social Democratic Association (ISDV). Its leaders, Semaun and Darsono, argued that capitalist imperialism had proletarianized Indonesian society and that the national and proletarian struggles thus coincided. . . . The PKI won wide support in Java and Sumatra, attracting the attention of the Dutch police. To maintain its élan and forestall repression, the party launched uprisings in Banten (1926) and West Sumatra (1927). . . . These uprisings were abortive and led the Dutch to suppress the party and exile many cadres to West New Guinea.

In 1935 [Communist leader] Musso established the Illegal PKI, which followed an antifascist line and remained underground until 1948. An aboveground party was established in 1945 and briefly led by Muhammad Jusuf, later by Alimin and Sardjono. It was subordinate to the underground party, and party members were active in several parties within the ruling Sayap Kiri ("left wing"). The PKI supported negotiations with the Dutch to ensure the Indonesian Republic's survival, but after the fall of Amir Sjarifuddin's cabinet in January 1948 it increasingly favored armed struggle by workers and peasants. In August 1948 the PKI emerged openly as leader of the Front Demokrasi Rakyat (People's Democratic Front) under Musso and Sjarifuddin but was suppressed militarily for its involvement in the Madiun Affair (September 1948) [when Communists were involved in a violent uprising].

After Madiun, the PKI, under Tan Ling Djie, resumed the strategy of working through front parties. This policy, however, was

In 1950 the PKI had explicitly abandoned revolutionary war in favor of a peaceful path to power through parliament and elections. This strategy had been thwarted in 1957, when Sukarno suspended parliamentary rule and began to construct his Guided Democracy, which emphasized balance and cooperation between the diverse ideological streams present in Indonesia.

discarded in 1951 by the new-generation leadership—D.N. Aidit, M.H. Lukman, Nyoto, and Sudisman—who rehabilitated the party politically by stressing its nationalist commitment and renouncing armed revolution. The party survived repression by the Sukiman government and expanded its membership by broadening its base to include the peasantry, especially through one of its affiliates, the Barisan Tani Indonesia (Indonesian Peasants' Front). It won 16.4 percent of the vote in the 1955 elections and later claimed three million members.

Although it obtained political protection from Sukarno by backing his program of Guided Democracy and emphasized that its primary enemy was Dutch and American capital, the PKI drew the hostility of many intellectuals for its insistence on ideological correctness. The PKI also angered civilian and military officials as a result of its attacks on corruption and privilege and alienated the rural elite (often associated with Muslim parties) because of its support of peasant interests, especially its unilateral actions (aksi sepihak) in 1964 to carry out an as yet unimplemented land reform law in Central and East Java.

After the 1965 Gestapu Affair [that is, the September 30 incident], army units and Muslim youth conducted a pogrom in which perhaps 400,000 PKI members and supporters died and 100,000 were jailed. The party was banned in March 1966 but briefly conducted guerrilla operations near Blitar, East Java, and in West Kalimantan. PKI exiles in Beijing, led by Jusuf Ajitoropo, later publicized a self-criticism (otokritik) condemning the Aidit leadership for alleged revisionism and announcing a new Maoist program advocating armed revolution.

"Partai Komunis Indonesia," Encyclopedia of Asian History. Charles Scribner's Sons, 1988. World History in Context. August 5, 2013.

The PKI, however, had recovered to become a dominant ideological stream. Leftist ideological statements permeated the public rhetoric of Guided Democracy, and the party appeared to be by far the largest and best-organized political movement in the country. Its influence not only encompassed the poor and disadvantaged but also extended well into military and civilian elites, which appreciated the party's nationalism and populism, its reputation for incorruptibility, and its potential as a channel of access to power. Yet the party had many enemies. Throughout Indonesia, the PKI had chosen sides in long-standing local conflicts and in so doing had inherited ancient enmities. It was also loathed by many in the army for its involvement in the 1948 Madiun Affair, a revolt against the Indonesian Republic during the war of independence against the Dutch. Although the party had many sympathizers in the armed forces and in the bureaucracy, it controlled no government departments and, more important, had no reliable access to weapons. Thus, although there were observers who believed that the ideological élan of the party and its strong mass base would sweep it peacefully into power after Sukarno, others saw the party as highly vulnerable to army repression. A preemptive strike against the anticommunist high command of the army appeared to be an attractive strategy, and indeed it seems that this was the path chosen by Aidit, who appears to have been acting on his own and without reference to other members of the party leadership.

In fact, the military opponents of the PKI had been hoping for some time that the communists would launch an abortive coup, believing that this would provide a pretext for suppressing the party. The September 30 Movement therefore played into their hands. There is evidence that Suharto knew in advance that a plot was afoot, but there is neither evidence nor a plausible account to support the theory . . . that the coup was an intelligence operation by Suharto to eliminate his fellow generals and compromise the PKI. Rather, Suharto and other conservative generals were ready to make the most of the opportunity which Aidit and the September 30 Movement provided.

Demonizing the PKI

The army's strategy was to portray the coup as an act of consummate wickedness and as part of a broader PKI plan to seize power. Within days, military propagandists had reshaped

Indonesian soldiers stand near the wreckage of a burning vehicle in the aftermath of the attempted coup in early October 1965. © Beryl Bernay/Getty Images.

the name of the September 30 Movement to construct the acronym GESTAPU, with its connotations of the ruthless evil of the Gestapo. They concocted a story that the kidnapped generals had been tortured and sexually mutilated by communist women before being executed, and they portrayed the killings of October 1 as only a prelude to a planned nationwide purge of anticommunists by PKI members and supporters. In lurid accounts, PKI members were alleged to have dug countless holes so as to be ready to receive the bodies of their enemies. They were also accused of having been trained in the techniques of torture, mutilation, and murder. The engagement of the PKI as an institution in the September 30 Movement was presented as fact rather than conjecture. Not only the party as a whole but also its political allies and affiliated organizations were portrayed as being guilty both of the crimes of the September 30 Movement and of conspiracy to commit further crimes on a far greater scale. At the same time, President Sukarno was portrayed as culpable for having tolerated the PKI within Guided Democracy. His effective powers were gradually circumscribed, and he was finally stripped of the presidency on March 12, 1967. General Suharto took over and installed a military-dominated, development-oriented regime known as the New Order, which survived until 1998.

In this context, the army began a purge of the PKI from Indonesian society. PKI offices were raided, ransacked, and burned. Communists and leftists were purged from government departments and private associations. Leftist organizations and leftist branches of larger organizations dissolved themselves. Within about two weeks of the suppression of the coup, the killing of communists began.

Remarkably few accounts of the killings were written at the time, and the long era of military-dominated government that followed in Indonesia militated against further reporting. The destruction of the PKI was greeted enthusiastically by the West, with *Time* magazine describing it as "The West's best news for years in Asia," and there was no international pressure on the military to halt or limit the killings. After the fall of Suharto in 1998, there was some attempt to begin investigation of the massacres, but these efforts were hampered by continuing official and unofficial anti-communism and by the pressure to investigate more recent human rights abuses. President Abdurrahman Wahid (1999–2001) apologized for the killings on behalf of his orthodox Muslim association, Nahdlatul Ulama, but many Indonesians continued to regard the massacres as warranted. As a result, much remains unknown about the killings.

The Killings

Many analyses of the massacres have stressed the role of ordinary Indonesians in killing their communist neighbors. These accounts have pointed to the fact that anticommunism became a manifestation of older and deeper religious, ethnic, cultural, and class antagonisms. Political hostilities were reinforced by more ancient enmities. Particularly in East Java, the initiative for some killings came from local Muslim leaders determined to extirpate an enemy whom they saw as infidel. Also important was the opaque political atmosphere of late Guided Democracy. Indonesia's economy was in serious decline, poverty was widespread, basic necessities were in short supply, semi-political criminal gangs made life insecure in many regions, and political debate was conducted with a bewildering mixture of venom and camaraderie. With official and public news sources entirely unreliable, people depended on rumor, which both sharpened antagonisms and exacerbated uncertainty. In these circumstances, the military's expert labeling of the PKI as the culprit in the events of October 1, and as the planner of still worse crimes, unleashed a wave of mass retaliation against the communists in which the common rhetoric was one of "them or us."

Accounts of the killings that have emerged in recent years, however, have indicated that the military played a key role in the killings in almost all regions. In broad terms, the massacres took place according to two patterns. In Central Java and parts of Flores and West Java, the killings took place as almost pure military operations. Army units, especially those of the elite para-commando regiment RPKAD, commanded by Sarwo Edhie, swept through district after district arresting communists on the basis of information provided by local authorities and executing them on the spot. In Central Java, some villages were wholly PKI and attempted to resist the military, but they were defeated and all or most villagers were massacred. In a few regions—notably Bali and East Java—civilian militias, drawn from religious groups (Muslim in East Java, Hindu in Bali, Christian in some other regions) but armed, trained, and authorized by the army, carried out raids themselves. Rarely did militias carry out massacres without explicit army approval and encouragement.

More common was a pattern in which party members and other leftists were first detained. They were held in police stations, army camps, former schools or factories, and improvised camps. There they were interrogated for information and to obtain confessions before being taken away in batches to be executed, either

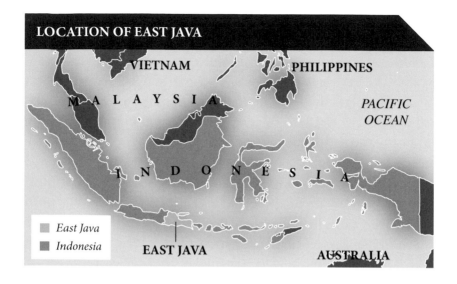

LOCATION OF EAST JAVA

by soldiers or by civilian militia recruited for the purpose. Most of the victims were killed with machetes or iron bars.

The killings peaked at different times in different regions. The majority of killings in Central Java were over by December 1965, while killings in Bali and in parts of Sumatra took place mainly in early 1966. Although the most intense killings were over by mid-March 1966, sporadic executions took place in most regions until at least 1970, and there were major military operations against alleged communist underground movements in West Kalimantan, Purwodadi (Central Java), and South Blitar (East Java) from 1967 to 1969.

Central and East Java

It is generally believed that the killings were most intense in Central and East Java, where they were fueled by religious tensions between *santri* (orthodox Muslims) and *abangan* (followers of a syncretic local Islam heavily influenced by pre-Islamic belief and practice). In Bali, class and religious tensions were strong; and in North Sumatra, the military managers of state-owned plantations had a special interest in destroying the power of the communist plantation workers' unions. There were pockets of intense killing, however, in other regions. The total number of victims to the end of 1969 is impossible to estimate reliably, but many scholars accept a figure of about 500,000. The highest estimate is 3,000,000.

Aidit, who went underground immediately after the failure of the coup, was captured and summarily executed, as were several other party leaders. Others, together with the military leaders of the September 30 Movement, were tried in special military tribunals and condemned to death. Most were executed soon afterward, but a few were held for longer periods, and the New Order periodically announced further executions. A few remained in jail in 1998 and were released by Suharto's successor, President B.J. Habibie.

It is important to note that Chinese Indonesians were not, for the most part, a significant group among the victims. Although Chinese have repeatedly been the target of violence in independent Indonesia, and although there are several reports of Chinese shops and houses being looted between 1965 and 1966, the vast majority of Chinese were not politically engaged and were expressly excluded from the massacres of communists in most regions.

US Involvement

Outside the capital, Jakarta, the army used local informants and captured party documents to identify its victims. At the highest level, however, the military also used information provided by United States intelligence sources to identify some thousands of people to be purged. Although the lists provided by the United States have not been released, it is likely that they included both known PKI leaders and others whom the American authorities believed to be agents of communist influence but who had no public affiliation with the party.

Alongside the massacres, the army detained leftists on a massive scale. According to official figures, between 600,000 and 750,000 people passed through detention camps for at least short periods after 1965, though some estimates are as high as 1,500,000. These detentions were partly adjunct to the killings—victims were detained prior to execution or were held for years as an alternative to execution—but the detainees were also used as a cheap source of labor for local military authorities. Sexual abuse of female detainees was common, as was the extortion of financial contributions from detainees and their families. Detainees with clear links to the PKI were dispatched to the island of Buru, in eastern Indonesia, where they were used to construct new agricultural settlements. Most detainees were released by 1978, following international pressure.

Ongoing Discrimination

Even after 1978, the regime continued to discriminate against former detainees and their families. Former detainees commonly had to report to the authorities at fixed intervals (providing opportunities for extortion). A certificate of non-involvement in the 1965 coup was required for government employment or employment in education, entertainment, or strategic industries. From the early 1990s, employees in these categories were required to be "environmentally clean," meaning that even family members of detainees born after 1965 were excluded from many jobs, and their children faced harassment in school. A ban on such people being elected to the legislature was lifted only in 2004. A ban on the teaching of Marxism-Leninism remains in place.

Although the 1948 United Nations Convention on Genocide does not acknowledge political victims as victims of genocide, the Indonesian case indicates that the distinction between victims defined by "national, ethnical, racial, or religious" identity on the one hand and political victims on the other may be hard to sustain. Indonesian national identity is defined politically, rather than by ethnicity or religion, so that the communist victims of 1965 and after, constituting a different political vision of Indonesia from that of their enemies, may be said by some to have constituted a national group.

VIEWPOINT 2

Lieutenant Colonel Untung Declares the September 30 Coup

Untung Syamsuri

Lieutenant Colonel Untung Syamsuri was an Indonesian military officer and one of the leaders of the 1965 coup attempt in Indonesia called the September 30 Movement. In the following viewpoint, he, or those speaking in his name, declares that the September 30 Movement has overthrown Indonesia's army generals and has taken President Sukarno under its protection. He also states that the government of Indonesia will continue on revolutionary principles. (The coup failed soon after this announcement was made; Untung was executed for treason in 1967.)

(Text as broadcast over the Djakarta radio at approximately 7:15 A.M. on the morning of October 1.)

On Thursday, September 30, 1965, a military move took place within the Army in the capital city of Djakarta which was aided by troops from other branches of the Armed Forces. The September 30th Movement, which is led by Lieutenant Colonel Untung, Commandant of a Battalion of the Tjakrabirawa, the personal bodyguard of President Sukarno, is directed against

Untung Syamsuri, "Initial Statement of Lieutenant Colonel Untung," as in *The Sukarno File, 1965–1967: Chronology of a Defeat*, ed. Antonie C.A. Dake. Brill Academic Publishers: 2006, pp. 289–291. Copyright © 2006 by Koninklijke BRILL NV. All rights reserved. Reproduced by permission.

The Character of Untung

After the Madiun uprising of 1948, in which Untung fought on the side of the Communists, his military career had been in eclipse for a period of years. In the West Irian Campaign of May 1962 [against the Dutch], however, he distinguished himself as commander of one of the two companies of the 454th Battalion that were air-dropped into Irian. As the hero of the campaign, he was soon promoted from captain to major, and from then on, his career was on the upswing. He was appointed commander of the 454th Battalion and, a few months before the coup, was given the prestigious assignment of battalion commander in the Tjakrabirawa Palace Guard. Only 40 years old in 1965, Untung had a promising future in the army at the time of the coup.

On 19 February 1963, on his return from Irian, he was presented with a medal by President Sukarno at an impressive ceremony on the lawn of Merdeka Palace in the presence of the diplomatic corps and high government officials. The major was clad in battle dress; behind him in similar array stood five companies from the guerrilla force. Following Untung's report, Sukarno pinned medals on his chest and those of his associate guerrilla leaders, amidst applause from the assembled public. A few days later, Sukarno

Generals who were members of the self-styled Council of Generals. A number of Generals have been arrested and important communications media and other vital installations have been placed under the control of the September 30th Movement, while President Sukarno is safe under its protection. Also a number of other prominent leaders in society, who had become targets of the action by the Council of Generals, are under the protection of the September 30th Movement.

Against the Council of Generals

The Council of Generals is a subversive movement sponsored by the CIA and has been very active lately, especially since President entertained the heroes with "an evening of merriment."

An Indonesian reporter who interviewed Untung shortly after his return from West Irian was struck by Untung's "display of sincere emotion.". . .

A quite different picture of Untung was given by a lieutenant who served under him in the Irian campaign. According to the lieutenant, Untung was very ambitious. When he was about to be dropped into Irian he was still a captain but was given the local rank of major for the occasion. He refused to jump until he had been given the insignia of his new rank, and so another major gave his up for Untung. According to Untung's fellow officer, Untung was known as an atheist, a loner, and cruel. On landing in Irian he abandoned one of his men in the jungle because he was disabled, on the grounds that it was better one should die than that all should be placed in harm's way. Although he prevented his men from buying transistor radios while in Irian, he himself brought back several, which he got by blackmailing some Chinese. Presumably, the truth about Untung's character lies somewhere between these two extremes. One thing that seems clear is that he tended to be puritanical and strict with his men.

Helen-Louise Hunter, Sukarno and the Indonesian Coup: The Untold Story. *Westport, CT: Praeger Security International, 2007, pp. 73–74.*

Sukarno was seriously ill in the first week of August of this year. Their hope that President Sukarno would die of his illness has not materialized.

Therefore, in order to attain its goal the Council of Generals had planned to conduct a show of force (*machtvertoon*) on Armed Forces Day, October 5 this year, by bringing troops from East, Central and West Java. With this large concentration of military power the Council of Generals had even planned to carry out a counter-revolutionary coup prior to October 5, 1965. It was to prevent such a counter-revolutionary coup that Lieutenant Colonel Untung launched the September 30th Movement which has proved a great success.

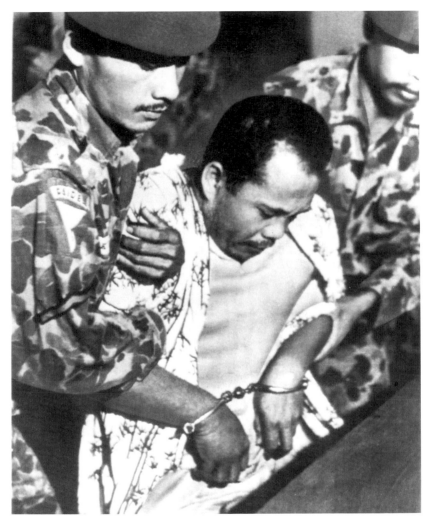

Untung bin Syamsuri (center), a leader of the attempted coup in Indonesia, is held by soldiers at a Jakarta prison on November 16, 1965. © AP Photo.

According to a statement obtained from Lieutenant Colonel Untung, the Commandant of the September 30th Movement, this movement is solely a movement within the Army directed against the Council of Generals which has stained the name of the Army and harbored evil designs against the Republic of Indonesia and President Sukarno. Lieutenant Colonel Untung personally considers this movement as an obligation for him as a member of the Tjakrabirawa which has the duty to protect the President and the Republic of Indonesia.

The Commandant of the September 30th Movement further explained that the action already taken against the Council of Generals in Djakarta will be followed by actions throughout Indonesia against agents and sympathizers of the Council of Generals in the regions. According to the statement of the Commandant of the September 30th Movement, as a follow-up action, an Indonesian Revolution Council will be established in the capital, while in the regions Provincial, District, Sub-District, and Village Revolution Councils will be established. Members of the Revolution Council will be composed of civilians and military personnel who fully support the September 30th Movement.

Political parties, mass organizations, newspapers, and periodicals may continue functioning, provided that within a time period which will be specified later they declare their loyalty to the Indonesian Revolution Council.

The Charms of the Revolution

The Indonesian Revolution Council which will be established by the September 30th Movement will consistently carry out the *Pantia Azimat Revolusi* [Charms of the Revolution], the decisions of the MPRS [Indonesian legislative branch], the decisions of the DPR-GR [Indonesian legislative House], and the decisions of the DPA [Indonesian Supreme Advisory Council]. The Indonesian Revolution Council will not change the Indonesian foreign policy, which is free and active and anti-nekolim [anti-neocolonialism], for the sake of peace in Southeast Asia and in the world. Also there will be no change of policy with regard to the Second Afro-Asian Conference and Conefo, as well as the confrontation against Malaysia [in which Indonesia opposed the creation of Malaysia]; KIAPMA [an anti-foreign military-bases conference], along with other international activities which have been scheduled to take place in Indonesia, will be held as planned.

As Commandant of the September 30th Movement, Lt. Colonel Untung called on the entire Indonesian people to continue to increase vigilance and fully assist the September 30th Movement in order to safeguard the Indonesian Republic from the wicked deeds of the Council of Generals and its agents, so that the Message of the People's Suffering can be fulfilled in the true sense of the word.

Lt. Colonel Untung appealed to all Army officers, non-commissioned officers and soldiers to be resolute and to act to eradicate completely the influence of the Council of Generals and its agents in the Army. Power-mad generals and officers who have neglected the lot of their men and who above the accumulated sufferings of their men have lived in luxury, led a gay life, insulted our women and wasted government funds, must be kicked out of the Army and punished accordingly. The Army is not for generals, but is the possession of all the soldiers of the Army who are loyal to the ideals of the revolution of August 1945. Lt. Colonel Untung thanked all troops of the Armed Forces outside the Army for their assistance in the purging of the Army and hoped that purges also will be carried out in the other branches of the Armed Forces against agents and sympathizers of the Council of Generals. Within a short time Commandant Lt. Colonel Untung will announce the First Decree concerning the Indonesian Revolution Council; other decrees will follow.

Djakarta, September 30, 1965.
Information Section of the September 30th Movement,
as broadcast over the Indonesian Radio in Djakarta.

An Anti-Communist Policy for Indonesia Is Presented to the Covert Oversight Committee

US State Department

The US State Department is the cabinet-level department charged with foreign affairs. In the following viewpoint, it outlines Indonesian policy for the 303 Committee, the National Security Council Committee charged with covert oversight. The State Department warns of increasing Communist influence in Indonesia and recommends funding propaganda, including false propaganda, in order to turn Indonesians against the Communist Party of Indonesia (PKI). The memo warns that this may prompt retaliation from President Sukarno, who has close ties with the PKI, but says that the risk is worth it.

Washington, February 23, 1965.
 SUBJECT
 Progress Report on [*less than 1 line of source text not declassified*] Covert Action in Indonesia

1. Summary
Since the summer of 1964, [*less than 1 line of source text not declassified*] has worked with the Department of State in formulat-

"Memorandum Prepared for the 303 Committee," State Department Website, February 23, 1965.

ing concepts and developing an operational program of political action in Indonesia aimed at bolstering the more moderate elements in the Indonesian political spectrum to counter the growing power of the Communist Party of Indonesia (PKI). This program has been coordinated in the Department of State with the Assistant Secretary for Far Eastern Affairs and with the U.S. Ambassador to Indonesia.

The aim of this political action program is to reduce the influence on Indonesian foreign and domestic policies of the PKI and the Government of Red China and to encourage and support existing non-Communist elements within Indonesia. The program envisages continuation of certain activities which have been undertaken previously on a developmental basis plus other new activities which appear now to offer promise of success if implemented on a coordinated and sustained basis. The main thrust of this program is designed to exploit factionalism within the PKI itself, to emphasize traditional Indonesian distrust of Mainland China and to portray the PKI as an instrument of Red Chinese imperialism. Specific types of activity envisaged include covert liaison with and support to existing anti-Communist groups, particularly among the [*less than 1 line of source text not declassified*], black letter operations, media operations, including possibly black radio, and political action within existing Indonesian organizations and institutions. The estimated annual cost of this program is [*less than 1 line of source text not declassified*]. These funds are available [*less than 1 line of source text not declassified*].

2. Problem

To counter the growing strength and influence of the Communist Party of Indonesia and Communist China over Indonesian foreign and domestic policies.

3. Factors Bearing on the Problem

One of the main factors bearing on the problem is the close affinity between the current objectives of Sukarno and Red China and the support provided to Sukarno by the PKI in contrast to the lack of coordination and common ground for action among the various anti-Communist elements within Indonesia.

a. Origin of the Requirement The requirement for a program of this type arose out of a series of discussions of the problem between Ambassador [Howard P.] Jones and the [*less than 1 line of source text not declassified*] and between Ambassador Jones and officials of the Department of State and the CIA in Washington.

b. Pertinent U.S. Policy Considerations The program is consistent with U.S. policy which seeks a stable, non-Communist Indonesia.

c. Operational Objectives Portray the PKI as an increasingly ambitious, dangerous opponent of Sukarno and legitimate nationalism and instrument of Chinese neo-imperialism.

Provide covert assistance to individuals and organizations capable of and prepared to take obstructive action against the PKI.

Encourage the growth of an ideological common denominator, within the framework of Sukarno's enunciated concepts, which will serve to unite non-Communist elements and create cleavage between the PKI and the balance of the Indonesian society.

Develop black and grey propaganda[1] themes and mechanisms for use within Indonesia and via appropriate media assets outside of Indonesia in support of the objectives of this program.

Identify and cultivate potential leaders within Indonesia for the purpose of ensuring an orderly non-Communist succession upon Sukarno's death or removal from office.

Identify, assess and monitor the activities of anti-regime elements for the purpose of influencing them to support a non-Communist successor regime.

d. Risks Involved Risks involved in this program include the possibility that were Sukarno to learn of its existence and to suspect that one of the objectives of the program is to weaken his control of Indonesian affairs, further deterioration of relations between Indonesia and the United States could result. An additional risk is the possibility that too blatant anti-PKI activity is likely to invite repressive measures on Sukarno's part, assisted by PKI attacks upon key anti-Communist leaders, with concomitant further disarray within the non-Communist groups. Nevertheless, it is believed that a program of this type should be attempted.

e. Funding The estimated annual cost of this program is [*less than 1 line of source text not declassified*]. Funds are available [*less than 1 line of source text not declassified*] to support this program.

f. Support Required from Other Agencies No support will be required from other agencies other than that normally deriving from Country Team cooperation in the field.

g. Timing of the Operation [*less than 1 line of source text not declassified*] has been developing active relationships with leading nationalist personalities [*1 line of source text not declassified*]. Through secure mechanisms some funds have been given to key personalities to bolster their ability and their resolve to continue their anti-Communist activities which essentially are in the U.S. direction. The proposed operational program will be carried out as soon as approved.

4. Coordination

This operational program has been approved by Assistant Secretary of State for Far Eastern Affairs and by the U.S. Ambassador to Indonesia. Continuing coordination of specific projects will be effected in Djakarta with the Principal Officer.

5. Recommendation

It is recommended that the 303 Committee [which oversees covert operations] approve this program.[2]

Notes:

1. Black propaganda is false information that claims to be from one side of a conflict (in this case the PKI) but is actually from the other side (in this case the CIA). Grey propaganda is propaganda without any identifiable source.

2. The 303 Committee approved this paper on March 4. [*text not declassified*] of the CIA took the opportunity to urge "a larger political design or master plan to arrest the Indonesian march into the Chinese camp" based on the Maphilindo concept [a proposed confederation of several Southeast Asian countries]. He argued a major effort was required to prevent the United States from being excluded from Indonesia, suggesting that the loss of a nation of 105 million to the "Communist camp" would make a victory in Vietnam of little meaning. [National Security Advisor] McGeorge Bundy stated that as a major political problem, Indonesia was receiving attention, but it "could not be settled in the 303 forum." (Ibid., 303 Committee Minutes, 3/5/65).

US Diplomats Formulate an Anti-Communist Response to the September 30 Incident

Marshall Green and George Ball

Marshall Green was a US diplomat and the ambassador to Indonesia in 1965. George Ball was a US State Department official during the John F. Kennedy and Lyndon Johnson administrations. In the following viewpoint, a telegram communication, Green and Ball discuss ways to help members of the military as they move against Sukarno and the Indonesian Communist Party (PKI) following the September 30 incident of 1965. They emphasize the desirability of undermining Sukarno and of keeping the public unaware of US involvement.

Telegram from the Embassy in Indonesia to the Department of State

Djakarta, October 5, 1965, 1435Z.

868. Ref: Embtel 852.

1. Events of the past few days have put PKI and pro-Communist elements very much on [the] defensive and they

Marshall Green and George Ball, "Telegram from the Embassy in Indonesia to the Department of State; Telegram from the Department of State to the Embassy in Indonesia," as in *Foreign Relations of the United States, 1964–1968, Volume XXVI: Indonesia, Malaysia, Singapore, Philippines*, eds. David S. Patterson and Edward C. Keefer. Washington, DC: United States Government Printing Office, 2000, pp. 307–310.

may embolden [the] army at long last to act effectively against Communists.

2. At [the] same time we seem to be witnessing what may be the passing of power from Sukarno's hands to a figure or figures whose identity is yet unknown, possibly bringing changes in national policy and posture in its wake.

3. Right now, our key problem is if we can help shape developments to our advantage, bearing in mind that events will largely follow their own course as determined by basic forces far beyond our capability to control.

4. [The] following guidelines may supply part of the answer to what our posture should be:

A. Avoid overt involvement as [the] power struggle unfolds.

B. Covertly, however, indicate clearly to key people in [the] army such as [Abdul Haris] Nasution and Suharto [who shortly took control of Indonesia] our desire to be of assistance where we can, while at [the] same time conveying to them our assumption that we should avoid [the] appearance of involvement or interference in any way.

C. Maintain and if possible extend our contact with [the] military.

D. Avoid moves that might be interpreted as [a] note of nonconfidence in [the] army (such as precipitately moving out our dependents or cutting staff).

E. Spread the story of PKI's guilt, treachery and brutality (this priority effort is perhaps [the] most needed immediate assistance we can give [the] army if we can find [a] way to do it without identifying it as solely or largely [a] US effort).

F. Support, through information output and such other means as becomes available to us, unity of Indonesian armed forces.

G. Bear in mind that Moscow and Peking are in basic conflict regarding Indonesia, and that [the]Soviet Union might find itself even more in line with our thinking than at present. This will be [the] subject of our next Country Team meeting and we may have specific recommendations for exploiting this phenomenon.

H. Continue to consult closely with friendly embassies (who take up much of our time and occasionally our facilities) extending our line of credit and enhancing our image generally through them as a constructive influence here.

I. Continue for [the] time being to maintain [a] low profile and be restrained about any apparent opportunities to rush in with new, overt programs (although [the] need for [a] stepped-up information effort will be great).

5. We will submit further recommendations as these seem to be appropriate to what will undoubtedly be [a] fast-moving or at least [an] uncertain situation for some time to come.

[Marshall] Green

Telegram from the Department of State to the Embassy in Indonesia

Washington, October 6, 1965, 7:39 P.M.
400. Ref Embtel 868.

1. Subject to comments on emphasis and discretion below, we are in basic agreement with policy guidelines set forth [in] para 4 reftel.

2. Reports of [the] October 6 Cabinet meeting just received via FBIS [Foreign Broadcast Information Service] make it clear Sukarno is attempting to reestablish status quo ante by raising bogey of imperialist exploitation [of] Indonesian differences and submerging [the] Army's vengeful hostility towards PKI in a closing of ranks to preserve national unity.

3. As you have brought out, [the] major question is whether [the] Army can maintain momentum [of] its offensive against PKI in [the] face [of] Sukarno's practiced political manipulations.

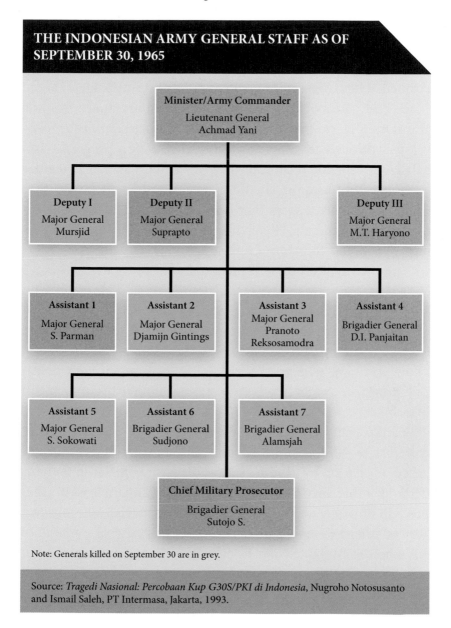

THE INDONESIAN ARMY GENERAL STAFF AS OF SEPTEMBER 30, 1965

Minister/Army Commander
Lieutenant General
Achmad Yani

Deputy I
Major General
Mursjid

Deputy II
Major General
Suprapto

Deputy III
Major General
M.T. Haryono

Assistant 1
Major General
S. Parman

Assistant 2
Major General
Djamijn Gintings

Assistant 3
Major General
Pranoto
Reksosamodra

Assistant 4
Brigadier General
D.I. Panjaitan

Assistant 5
Major General
S. Sokowati

Assistant 6
Brigadier General
Sudjono

Assistant 7
Brigadier General
Alamsjah

Chief Military Prosecutor
Brigadier General
Sutojo S.

Note: Generals killed on September 30 are in grey.

Source: *Tragedi Nasional: Percobaan Kup G30S/PKI di Indonesia*, Nugroho Notosusanto and Ismail Saleh, PT Intermasa, Jakarta, 1993.

4. Sukarno, Subandrio [Foreign Minister] and PKI sympathizers in Cabinet will be alert to any evidence substantiating their charges that NEKOLIM [neocolonialists] will attempt to exploit [the] situation. We believe it essential that we not give

Sukarno and company [the] opportunity [to] claim that they [are] about to be attacked by NEKOLIM and that we not give Subandrio and the PKI citable public evidence that [the] USG [United States Government] supports [the] Army against them.

5. [The] Army clearly needs no material assistance from us at this point. Over [the] past years inter-service relationships developed through training programs, civic action programs and MILTAG [Military Technical Advisory Group] as well as regular assurances to Nasution, should have established clearly in [the] minds [of] Army leaders that [the] U.S. stands behind them if they should need help. [Reference your] paras 4 b and c [we] believe we should therefore exercise extreme caution in contacts with the Army lest our well-meaning efforts to offer assistance or steal their resolve may in fact play into [the] hands of Sukarno and Subandrio. In particular, given Nasution's apparent present emotional state and precariousness [we] do not believe it wise for you to attempt direct contact with him unless he seeks it, but know you have reliable indirect access to him through politically conscious senior officers who [are] routinely in contact with Mission.

6. We plan and are already carrying out VOA [Voice of America, a US radio broadcast] and information programs based on citation [of] Indonesian sources and official statements without at this stage injecting U.S. editorializing. At least in [the] present situation we believe ample such material pointing fingers at [the] PKI and playing up [the] brutality of September 30¹ rebels is available from Radio Djakarta and Indo press, but we will look at [the] situation again if in [the] coming days or weeks these sources dry up. Similar coverage will be given by [the] VOA to Indo situation in key broadcasts other than to Indonesia.

7. [Reference your] para 4 d, [we] agree that precipitate evacuation [is] undesirable, but it is essential that you start moving out dependents and non-essential staff as commercial space becomes available on any carrier to any point. . . .

8. Will look forward to further Embassy recommendations as to how we should proceed.

[George] Ball

Note:

1. The September 30 Movement was a Communist takeover attempt. It failed, but several generals were murdered.

Sukarno Is Forced from Power

Ottawa Citizen

The Ottawa Citizen *is a Canadian newspaper. In the following viewpoint, the paper reports on the fall of Sukarno, who was finally pushed from power by Suharto in 1967. The viewpoint discusses Sukarno's popularity in Indonesia and his courage in fighting for Indonesian independence against the Dutch. It says that his regime was rife with corruption, and that he damaged Indonesia's economy by nationalizing industries that Indonesia itself did not have the capacity to develop.*

President Sukarno led Indonesia to independence from Dutch rule and for 21 years maintained one-man rule, mainly by the dint of spellbinding oratory.

The fall from power of the flamboyant, magnetic Sukarno came after a year of bitter political feuding with Gen. Suharto, the army strongman who crushed Indonesia's Communists after their coup attempt failed in 1965.

But the government leaders who brought about his downfall moved cautiously for fear a showdown might bring on civil war.

Sukarno (left), the Indonesian president, surrendered executive powers to General Suharto on February 22, 1967. © AP Photo.

People's Hero

Sukarno, 65, was revered by most of Indonesia's 100,000,000 people for years. They hung on his every word and massed by the thousands for a glimpse of him.

It is true Sukarno gave the Indonesians heart and courage in the difficult days of the struggle for independence, but later he gave Indonesia incredible chaos.

Until a year ago, he was president, premier, supreme commander of the armed forces, great leader of the revolution and mouthpiece of Indonesia.

Then all of these powers were chipped away gradually by the military after the Communist bid for power failed and Sukarno himself was implicated by testimony of coup leaders placed on trial as having a hand in the attempt.

Largely because of Sukarno and the immense corruption that surrounded him, Indonesia remains a broken nation largely

Sukarno's Foreign Policy

Indonesian foreign policy in recent years has displayed two sharply contrasting faces. Under Sukarno in the first half of the 1960s, Indonesia aspired to lead an international anti-imperialist front. Sukarno condemned the prevailing international system as an exploitative order in which the "old established forces" (OLDEFOS) of the world sought to keep the "new emerging forces" (NEFOS) in subjugation. Warning that aid from the OLDEFOS was but another device to limit the independence of the NEFOS, he exalted self-reliance and told the United States to "go to hell with your aid." As Indonesia's economy stagnated, Sukarno filled his people's ears with stirring oratory, hammering away at the theme that real independence was possible only through an all-out confrontation with the forces of exploitation.

Under Soeharto since 1966, however, Indonesian foreign policy has eschewed flamboyance and oriented itself to the search for Western economic aid and capital investment.

Franklin B. Weinstein, Indonesian Foreign Policy and the Dilemma of Dependence: From Sukarno to Soeharto. *Singapore: Equinox Press, 2007, p. 19.*

of peasants, empty of industry, department stores and modern housing.

Indonesia is rich in oil, rubber, copper, tin and diamonds. But these resources were left largely untouched after Sukarno under Communist influence nationalized most of these industries. Indonesia simply did not have the technicians to run them.

Sukarno was born near Surabaya in East Java on June 6, 1901. As a youth he was good in languages but was not an outstanding student. In high school his flair for oratory developed.

In 1920 he went to the Bandung Technical Institute where he studied engineering. Whether he graduated is still a matter of debate.

While still in school he married and divorced one young girl, then married the widowed daughter of a wealthy Javanese family.

She was several years his elder.

By 1928 the Indonesian Nationalist Organization was formed, and Sukarno, at age 27, was its chairman.

He was launched on his career as a nationalist and revolutionary leader.

Jailed several times by the Dutch colonialists, he survived to return and inflame the Indonesians with the idea of independence.

His Chance

The opportunity became real with the arrival of the Japanese occupation forces in 1942. Although often accused of collaborating with the Japanese, Sukarno appeared to be attempting to cope with the situation until he could move his nationalist forces again.

The defeat of the Japanese brought the return of the Dutch, but Sukarno had already declared Indonesia independent.

Nearly five years of bitter guerrilla war followed before the Dutch were forced out.

Shortly before then, Sukarno divorced his second wife and married Fatmawati. He had four children by her. Then in 1954 he took his fourth wife, Martini. She was only his second official wife. He later took two more official wives, the maximum under Moslem law.

Suharto Dies

Shawn Donnan and John Aglionby

*Shawn Donnan is world trade editor and John Aglionby is a se-
nior reporter at the* Financial Times. *In the following viewpoint,
they report on Suharto's death and assess his legacy. On the one
hand, they say, Suharto brought stability and economic growth to
Indonesia and dampened ethnic and religious tensions. However,
they say, his regime was repressive. He encouraged the slaughter
of hundreds of thousands in the 1965 anti-Communist purges, as
well as massacres of separatists in East Timor in the 1990s. His
rule ended in economic chaos amidst the Asian economic crisis of
1997—a crisis, the authors conclude, that his corrupt rule left his
country ill-prepared to weather.*

Suharto, the former Indonesian strongman who died Sunday
[January 2008] at the age of 86, was reviled as the man who
brought Indonesia to its knees when his 32-year rule ended in a
frenzy of violence, corruption and economic collapse.

Shawn Donnan and John Aglionby, "Obituary: Indonesia's Suharto," *Financial Times,*
January 27, 2008. From The Financial Times © The Financial Times Limited 2008. All rights
reserved. Cengage Learning is solely responsible for providing this abridged version of the
original article and The Financial Times Limited does not accept any liability for the accuracy or quality of the version.

Stability, Corruption, Oppression Ruled

Yet in the chaotic years after he left office in May 1998 and retired to his family compound in the leafy streets of Jakarta's diplomatic precinct, most Indonesians have come to view his rule with more nostalgia than anger. Whatever misdeeds his three decades of rule brought, whatever curtailments of human rights they saw, Suharto's rule brought stability and a welcome prosperity to a turbulent and impoverished country.

In the Javanese tradition, he simply had one name—Suharto. To most Indonesians he was "Pak" (Father) Harto. But to the international community, his reputation will forever be over-shadowed by his legendary corruption. When Transparency International, the anti-corruption campaign group, published in 2004 its list of the most corrupt political leaders of the prior two decades, it put Suharto at the top. His estimated take over three decades in power was up to $35bn.

Suharto's achievements were significant, nonetheless. Over the 30 years leading up to the Asian financial crisis in 1997, Indonesia achieved an average economic growth of 7 per cent. Suharto opened the economy to the outside world, and attracted billions in foreign investment.

His rule—oppressive as it was—also brought a measure of harmony to a multi-ethnic society. It kept the threat of extremist Islam in check in the world's largest Muslim nation. Under his patronage the country's ethnic Chinese came to dominate the country's economy, even if they were accorded only second-class status as citizens.

He Was Ruthless

Those achievements were punctuated by severe shortcomings. Quintessentially Javanese in character, Suharto was an inward-looking leader. Even after his downfall and amid threats of pros-ecution he continued to live on Jalan Cendana, a street in central Jakarta. To some that seemed the ultimate symbol of Suharto's impunity and the power his family continued to wield, even in a democratic Indonesia.

During his rule his six children became notorious for profiting from everything from toll roads to the issuing of driving licences. Yet after his fall only one—his youngest son, "Tommy"—was sent to jail.

Suharto himself escaped criminal prosecution after court-appointed doctors ruled that two strokes had left permanent brain damage that made him unfit to stand trial. To circumvent this, the government of President Susilo Bambang Yudhoyono launched in 2007 a civil suit against him and one of the foundations he established. They are being sued for $1.54bn, for allegedly stealing $440m of state funds.

Although Suharto liberalised the economy, he never nurtured the institutional strengths needed to underpin it. Regulation of the banking sector was weak, and the country was ill-equipped to withstand the economic crisis that hastened the end of his tenure.

He dealt with opposition in a ruthless way, using the army in brutal suppression of separatist uprisings in East Timor, Aceh and West Papua, all places where violence abounded and abuse of human rights was flagrant. Under his rule Indonesia was notionally a democracy, but parliament was little more than a rubber stamp. Political activity was circumscribed and free expression suppressed.

Genocide and New Order

Born on June 8, 1921, into poverty in the village of Kemusu Angamulja, in central Java, Suharto had a troubled early family life. He joined the Dutch colonial army at 19, and later became a sergeant. After the Japanese invasion in the second world war and subsequent Dutch surrender, he became a militia commander in the Japanese-run forces. When they were in turn defeated, he joined the Indonesian nationalist forces backing the independence movement of Sukarno, who became the country's first president, and fought against the Dutch during the 1945–50 war of independence.

It was an alleged coup attempt against President Sukarno in 1965 that gave Suharto his chance of power. Indonesia's economy was in tatters and the army was irritated by Sukarno's overtures to the Indonesian communist party, or PKI. The communists were blamed for an attempted coup in September that saw the murder of six top generals and a junior officer. To shore up his power, Sukarno pretended it was a minor incident and appointed Suharto, then still a largely unknown general, as head of the military.

But the killings led to an orgy of bloodshed that saw murder squads of Islamic activists and soldiers massacring communists, ethnic Chinese and anyone suspected of left-wing tendencies, killing an estimated 1m people. Many historians now believe the slaughter had the approval of Suharto, just as some believe he had a hand in the supposed coup.

As Sukarno clung to power, Suharto built support within the military. By March 1966 he had forced Sukarno to sign over effective control of Indonesia to him and his "New Order", and a year later Suharto took over the presidency.

The new head of state was a striking contrast to the flamboyant Sukarno. If Sukarno leaned a post-colonial left, Suharto was fervently anti-communist, imprisoning thousands of suspected communists and ensuring that even their grandchildren would suffer discrimination as long as he ruled. Whereas Sukarno built close relations with China, Suharto sought a more intimate relationship with the US.

His rule did not go without challenge. In 1974, he clamped down on generals who attempted to force him out of office because of student protests against corruption, rising prices and the influx of foreign investors who displaced indigenous businesses.

East Timor Subjected to Brutality

Suharto also became the focus of international controversy. In 1975 he ordered the invasion of East Timor after the sudden collapse of Portuguese authority, and subjected the territory to a long and brutal counter-insurgency campaign. That came to a head in 1991 with a massacre of demonstrators in the capital, Dili. To Suharto's consternation a Timorese bishop, Carlos Belo, and the country's current prime minister, Jose Ramos Horta, an independence leader at the time, were given a joint Nobel peace prize in 1996. But East Timor was one subject on which Suharto was adamant. Only after he was ousted and after the deaths in 1999 of some 1,400 people in the months leading up to and following a United Nations-organised referendum did Jakarta cede control of the territory.

During the 1980s Suharto took steps to reduce the military's role in government. But as the economy became more open and growth accelerated, so pressure for political liberalisation mounted. The ruling elite resisted, arguing that Indonesia had fused traditional culture with a modern approach to produce its own brand of democracy.

Yet the manifest corruption of his regime fed mounting opposition. The death of his wife, Siti Hartinah, in 1996, and the onset of an economic crisis throughout the region in 1997 left him increasingly isolated. In 1998, the year of his downfall, the economy shrank 13.7 per cent, one of the steepest contractions ever witnessed.

Suharto's legacy remains a subject of passionate debate amongst the people he ruled. He led Indonesia out of chaos and built an economic tiger out of a turbulent, multi-ethnic nation. But the rule that began in chaos also ended in chaos, aggravated by the corruption he condoned and even encouraged. In the end, he was the architect of his own demise.

PKI Survivors Still Face Stigma in Indonesia

Alexandra Di Stefano Pironti

Alexandra Di Stefano Pironti is a reporter for IPS. *In the following viewpoint, she reports that those persecuted and tortured in 1965 and its aftermath continue to face discrimination and hardship. Pironti says that those who were placed in detention were marked even after they were released. They were often unable to get jobs, were rejected by their families, and continue to face hostility and prejudice. Indonesian textbooks continue to deny the atrocities of 1965, and organizations that participated have not acknowledged the crimes, Pironti adds. The former prisoners, she concludes, want their names cleared and their suffering acknowledged.*

If the caste system existed in Indonesia the 10 elderly people who live in Jakarta's Jalan Kramat would surely be untouchables: for decades they and their families have been banned from jobs and access to education and, until 2005, their identity cards marked them as former political prisoners.

A Blood-Soaked History

They are survivors of the 1965–66 military crackdown on the now outlawed Indonesian Communist Party (PKI), during which time between 500,000 and three million people were massacred and thousands tortured and imprisoned without trial.

Ostracized since General Suharto ousted independence leader Sukarno in 1965 and began a 32-year dictatorship marked by anti-communist zeal, the former prisoners interviewed by IPS at the old two-story villa in downtown Jakarta offered a string of traumatic tales that give but a glimpse into a blood-soaked chapter of Indonesian history that many have chosen to forget.

Pak Rosidi, an 86-year-old former agricultural engineer who graduated from the University of New England in Australia, recalled in perfect English the horrors he suffered until 1980 in the notorious detention camp of Buru Island, where a recent investigation uncovered conditions that had amounted to slavery.

"I was dismissed from my job at the Department of Agriculture in 1970 and arrested because I was Sukarnist, not a communist," he said.

"I am speechless about my years in prison. I was beaten, and continuously electrocuted for three hours at a time during those years," the soft-spoken Rosidi recounted.

"I had three children and I was married before I went to jail, but my wife rejected me when I returned," he added.

Strained family ties are a common theme in the stories of former prisoners, at a time when fear pushed children to turn against their parents in a bid to escape a life of discrimination.

Like many others, Rosidi faced difficulties making a living after jail because his identity card was marked "Ex Tapol" (former prisoner). That barred people like him from decent jobs, and banned them from careers in law, politics and the military. Their children were denied access to university education.

Ibu Snanto, now 85 and a housemate of Pak Rosidi, was in jail from 1966 to 1975 because her husband was a communist party member.

Indonesian Communists work in the yard of Salemba prison in Jakarta, Indonesia, in 1966.
© Co Rentmeester/Time & Life Pictures/Getty Images.

"My husband was the communist and I was only a housewife, but they arrested me and I was often electrocuted and sexually abused. I suffer from heart problems and trauma because of those years," she told IPS.

The Legacy of 1965

The massacres started against the backdrop of the Cold War on Oct. 1, 1965, when a group inside the armed forces calling itself the "Thirtieth of September Movement" kidnapped and killed six senior army generals, allegedly to prevent a coup against Sukarno, who was sympathetic to the PKI.

How many were killed and tortured, and the number who were imprisoned or are still alive, is not clear.

"We have spent two years of inquiry to find the numbers of people killed; but we cannot conduct validation, we haven't had help from military officials," Nur Kholis, a senior executive of the official Indonesian National Commission on Human Rights (Komnas HAM), told IPS.

In the first official report of its kind—released last July and based on interviews with 349 former prisoners—Komnas HAM acknowledged that "gross human rights violations" had taken place during the purge, including "murder, slavery, torture, sexual abuse, disappearances, cleansing, forced displacement and persecution."

The report recommends that the government of Indonesia, the world's most-populous Muslim nation, launch a national reconciliation process, and that the attorney general prosecute those found to be responsible for the crimes.

Kholis recounted to IPS the story of a witness in South Sumatra Island who saw army soldiers push 100 half-starved prisoners into the sea.

He also recounted the tale of a woman survivor in the city of Medan in North Sumatra Island who was forced to lie down naked while soldiers pushed bunches of lit matches into her vagina.

Ongoing Repression and Denial

Details of the anti-communist massacres are not found in Indonesian schoolbooks, and communism remains banned to this day. As recently as 2008, police summoned a group of artists in Bali to court for using symbols of the communist party during an exhibition.

Although Indonesia started its path to democracy in 1998 after Suharto was ousted as president, the current president, Susilo Bambang Yudhoyono, also a retired army general, has also been reluctant to re-open old wounds.

Meanwhile, the 10 former prisoners living on Jalan Kramat want nothing more than to have their names cleared of any wrongdoing.

"I want the stigma to be taken off us and recognition that the government says that we are good people," 87-year old Ibu Pujiati, who spent 14 years in jail after 1965 for being a labor activist, told IPS.

Australian university professor Robert Cribb, who has written extensively about Indonesia's recent history, believes that the government's refusal to acknowledge the suffering of victims has had a "profound effect" on the former prisoners.

"They have not only suffered discrimination, but they have been portrayed as unreliable citizens. Things that they believed in have been portrayed as evil," Cribb told IPS.

The biggest Muslim organization in Indonesia, Nahdlatul Ulama (NU), whose members took part in the persecution and killing of suspected communists alongside the military, believes that the former prisoners are best forgotten.

"They should not look for compensation. The conflict should be forgotten," As'ad Said Ali, a senior NU official, told IPS.

He justified the killings and persecution as "human nature," saying the massacres were driven by "revenge" for previous deadly conflicts between the PKI and NU.

"We don't like revenge because everything depends on God, but we want official rehabilitation for all of us," said former prisoner Ibu Snanto, eliciting nods from fellow victims at the Jalan Kramat home.

The poetry of former prisoner Putu Oka Sukanta succinctly paints those years as a time "when human life was as cheap as a gutter rat's."

Seventy-three-year-old Sukanta describes Leftists as being "hunted down by hungry dogs." Although never tried, he was jailed for 10 years for belonging to the cultural organization Lekra, which was affiliated to the communist party.

Indonesia's Collective Amnesia

Endy Bayuni

Endy Bayuni is the chief editor of the Jakarta Post, *Indonesia's leading English-language newspaper. In the following viewpoint, he discusses a new official Indonesian human rights report, which details the massive killings, torture, and abuse perpetrated by the Indonesian government during the period 1965–1966. Bayuni hopes the report will lead Indonesia to acknowledge past wrongs and perhaps establish a truth and reconciliation committee. However, he notes that Indonesian newspapers barely mentioned the report, and that most Indonesians have tried to forget the abuses of 1965. He says that the refusal to confront the past helps sustain Indonesia's culture of impunity from justice for the powerful.*

A new official report declaring the purge of communists in the 1960s in Indonesia to be a crime against humanity may be a historic milestone, but the muted public reaction suggests that this tragic episode has almost been wiped from the nation's collective memory.

On Monday, the National Commission on Human Rights, an independent state body, released its findings from a four-year investigation. The commission concludes that the army-led campaign amounted to a gross violation of human rights. It urged the government to prosecute the perpetrators and compensate victims and survivors. It also called upon President Susilo Bambang Yudhoyono to issue a public apology. But the report failed to generate much public interest, if the reaction of the country's major newspapers is any indication. They either ignored the story or buried it in the inside pages—which made for a jarring contrast to the hysterical headlines devoted to shooting in faraway Denver last weekend. But then the mainstream media have always been complicit in the conspiracy of silence over the killings, whether knowingly or out of ignorance.

The killing campaign in 1965 and 1966 was unleashed after an abortive coup against President Sukarno in October 1965 that the army blamed on the Indonesian Communist Party (PKI). Although the massacre happened on Sukarno's watch, he had by then become a lame-duck president. The report instead put the blame squarely on the Command for the Restoration of Security and Order led by General Soeharto, who went on to become president in 1967. The commission's recommendation only says that those most responsible should be prosecuted, though it gives no specific names.

In spite of its massive scale, the killing campaign has been shrouded in mystery. No one—the Human Rights Commission included—has ever been able to put a figure on how many were killed. Estimates range from a conservative 200,000 to as many as three million, a figure once boastingly cited by Sarwo Edhie Wibowo, who headed the military campaign at the time as chief of the army's Special Forces.

The Soeharto regime banned any discussion of the entire episode, including the massacre and the circumstances surrounding the transfer of power. For more than three decades, only the military's version of history was allowed to circulate. The veil of silence was lifted only some years after Soeharto stepped down in 1998.

Hundreds of victims of the 1965 massacre of Communists are buried in this Boyolal graveyard photographed in 2008. © Adek Berry/AFP/Getty Images.

Official history books today still treat the episode as an attempt by the PKI, then the world's largest communist party in a non-communist state, to grab power. They make no mention of the ensuing massacre of party members, their sympathizers and relatives, and even many innocent bystanders, or the harsh treatments meted out to the survivors in the aftermath of the killings.

The report, the most detailed study ever carried out on the massacre, lists the types of crimes committed, including murder, slavery, forced disappearances, limits to physical freedom, torture, rape, persecution, and forced prostitution. It also says the killing was widespread across most major islands in the archipelago, and not confined to Java, Sumatra, and Bali, as had been widely believed. The study also identified at least 17 mass graves where the victims were buried.

Although Indonesians who went through the period are aware of the killings, most have turned a blind eye, and many have even managed to erase them from memory. They accepted the official version that the military had saved Indonesia from communism, and, by logical conclusion, that Soeharto and his military cohorts were the heroes of the day. Time will tell how far the report will go to break these long years of the conspiracy of silence about the killings, and whether it will succeed in jolting the nation out of its collective amnesia. The report also calls for the establishment of a truth and reconciliation commission to look into the tragedy.

Scholars attempting to study the killings say that many of the perpetrators and the surviving victims have refused to be interviewed for events that they said were too traumatic to recount. A few, however, have been brave enough to break their silence, as captured in the film documentary *40 Years of Silence—An Indonesian Tragedy.* President Susilo Bambang Yudhoyono, for whom the report was prepared, responded positively by ordering the office of the attorney general to look into the recommendations, including considering the prosecution of those most responsible for the killings. His office has also said that the president is considering an official apology on behalf of the state for all the human rights violations committed against its own citizens.

All the key players in the killing campaign, however, are dead: Soeharto died in 2008, his deputy Admiral Sudomo this past April, and Sarwo Edhie, in 1989. It will be interesting to see how far the Indonesian military, or President Yudhoyono for that matter, are prepared to see their seniors tried in absentia or be dragged through the dirt in the event that the truth and reconciliation commission is formed. Yudhoyono, a military general himself, is the son-in-law of Sarwo Edhie.

Many human rights activists have their doubts. They note that a report by the same commission about the mass rape of Chinese Indonesians during a riot in 1998 never received any follow-up from the office of the attorney general.

The release of the report was hailed as a milestone by a handful of victims and survivors who had been seeking justice all these years. For most Indonesians, it was a non-event. In one of the rare public reactions to the report, Priyo Budi Santoso, a senior politician from the Golkar Party, said that wallowing in the past was unproductive for the nation. "It is better if we move forward," said Priyo, whose party provided the political machine that sustained Soeharto in power for more than three decades.

Tragically, he probably spoke for most of the people in this country.

Anyone wondering why the systemic culture of impunity, and with it the culture of violence, are so notoriously strong in Indonesia, may have found the answer this week. They are deeply embedded, along with the nation's collective amnesia.

CHAPTER 2

Controversies Surrounding the Indonesian Genocide of 1965

Chapter Exercises

SELECTED 20TH-CENTURY GENOCIDE DEATH TOLLS

Genocide	Dates	Estimated Death Toll
Nazi Holocaust (Hitler)	1939–1945	13 million
Holodomor in Ukraine (Stalin)	1932–1933	7–10 million
Khmer Rouge Killings in Cambodia (Pol Pot)	1975–1978	2 million
Turkish Genocide of Armenians	1915–1923	1.5 million
Indonesian Purge of Communists (Suharto)	1965–1966	500,000–1 million
Indonesian Occupation of East Timor (Suharto)	1975–1999	100,000–180,000

Sources: "The Holocaust Death Toll," *Telegraph*, January 26, 2005. www.telegraph.co.uk/news; "Holodomor," Consulate General of Ukraine in San Francisco. www.ukrainesf.com; "Cambodian Genocide," World Without Genocide. http://worldwithoutgenocide.org; "Frequently Asked Questions About the Armenian Genocide," Armenian-Genocide.org. www.armenian-genocide.org; and Colum Lynch and Ellen Nakashima, "E. Timor Atrocities Detailed," *Washington Post*, January 21, 2006. www.washington post.com.

1. Analyze the Table

Question 1: Which was the earliest atrocity of those listed above? Which was the most recent?

Question 2: In which genocide listed were the most people killed per year? In which were the least people killed per year?

Question 3: Which of the genocides above occurred concurrently?

2. Writing Prompt

Write a persuasive essay arguing either that the September 30 incident was part of a dangerous planned Communist takeover of Indonesia or that it was not.

3. Group Activity

Form groups and debate the following statement: The United States aided and encouraged the Indonesian massacre, and officials involved should be tried for war crimes.

C.I.A. Tie Asserted in Indonesia Purge

Michael Wines

Michael Wines is currently the China bureau chief for the New York Times. *In the following viewpoint, he reports that US officials deny CIA involvement in the Indonesian killings. Interviewees admit that lists were made and given to the Indonesian government. But, they say, these lists were made by one official and were not approved by the CIA as a whole. Officials also say the lists did not contain classified material and that they were not used by the Indonesian military to target Communists. The military, officials say, had plenty of targets for murder already and had no trouble identifying and massacring Communists without CIA help.*

A dispute has developed over a report that 25 years ago, United States officials supplied up to 5,000 names of Indonesian Communists to the Indonesian Army, which was then engaged in a campaign to wipe out the Communist Party in that country.

The House Intelligence Committee plans to investigate the report, which said that State Department and Central Intelligence Agency officials who served in Jakarta "described in lengthy interviews how they aided Indonesian Army leader Suharto" in his attack on the Indonesian Communist Party.

Gen. Suharto, now Indonesia's President, took control of the Government in October 1965, days after Communist insurgents launched an unsuccessful coup and killed six senior military officials. His army later encouraged and joined in a nationwide massacre of known and suspected Communists, which the C.I.A. has said claimed 250,000 lives before it ended in early 1966.

The article, distributed by the Washington-based States News Service on May 17, first appeared in The *Spartanburg* (S.C.) *Herald-Journal* on May 19, and has been published by other papers, including The *Washington Post*, in somewhat abridged form.

The author of the article, Kathy Kadane, quoted Robert J. Martens, who from 1963 to 1966 was a political officer at the United States Embassy in Jakarta, as saying that he had headed an embassy group of State Department and Central Intelligence Agency officers who for two years compiled lists of as many as 5,000 Communist Party members and sympathizers.

He was quoted as saying that the lists were turned over to an aide to the Indonesian Foreign Minister, who was known as an anti-Communist, once the massacre of Communists and others had begun.

The article also said that approval for the release of the names came from the top officials at the Embassy, including Ambassador Marshall Green.

Release of a List: Who Approved It?
There is no question that a list of names was provided to the Indonesians. The dispute has focused on whether the decision to turn over the names was that of an individual American Embassy officer, or was coordinated with the Central Intelligence Agency and approved by senior embassy officers.

Also, there is some disagreement over the significance of the action—whether the turning over of several thousand names was important information for the Indonesian Army.

Mr. Martens, who is retired from the Foreign Service and now lives in Maryland, acknowledged in an interview that he had passed the lists of names to the Indonesians. But he contended in a letter to the editor of The *Washington Post* that "I and I alone decided to pass those 'lists' to the non-Communist forces."

"I neither sought nor was given permission to do so by Ambassador Marshall Green or any other embassy official," he said in the letter.

"I also categorically deny that C.I.A. or any other classified material was turned over by me. Furthermore, I categorically deny that I 'headed an embassy group that spent two years compiling the lists.' No one, absolutely no one, helped me compile the lists in question."

He said in the letter that the lists were gathered entirely from the Indonesian Communist press and were available to everyone.

Mr. Green, who later became Assistant Secretary of State for East Asian and Pacific Affairs, called the Kadane account "garbage."

"There are instances in the history of our country, and specifically in the Far East, where our hands are not as clean, and where we have been involved," he said in Washington, where he lives in retirement. "But in this case we certainly were not."

Ms. Kadane said tape-recorded interviews support "every point of the story that was published," and the editor of States News Service, Leland Schwartz, said: "The news service stands behind the story and we feel that there is no question that what we said took place, took place. This comes from principals at the time."

Responding to a *New York Times* reporter's request, States News Service, which provides articles on Federal Government activities to local and regional newspapers, furnished transcripts of several key interviews used to prepare the article. They appear ambiguous on the central accusation: that Mr. Green and others approved releasing to the Indonesians a list of Communist Party members.

Muslim students in Jakarta protest after the attempted coup and demand the Communist Party be banned, in October 1965. © Carol Goldstein/Hulton Archive/Getty Images.

What Was US Role in Frenzied Killing?

The Indonesian coup attempt and the massacre occurred against a backdrop of political intrigue and virulent anti-Americanism in Jakarta, where the Government was then controlled by a charismatic pro-Communist dictator, President Sukarno. Mr. Sukarno had actively supported the three million-member Indonesian Communist Party, also known as the P.K.I., as a counterweight to General Suharto's growing influence as head of the military.

In October 1965, one day after a coup attempt by Communist forces was beaten back by General Suharto, Communist forces killed six senior military officers. In response, army units marched into Communist strongholds and, joined by anti-Communist civilians, began a frenzied round of killing. Mr. Sukarno retained titular control for another six months before being ousted by General Suharto.

In an interview, Mr. Martens said he told Ms. Kadane that he acted without approval because he wanted to avoid embassy red tape at what he believed was a critical time.

"I felt it necessary and useful to provide people standing up to this Communist takeover the means to understand what was happening," Mr. Martens said. "If we had any purpose in the world except to be bureaucrats, that was the sort of thing I felt we ought to be doing."

Ms. Kadane agrees that Mr. Martens told her that he acted alone, but contends that Mr. Green and two other officials then at the United States Embassy—the deputy chief of mission, Jack Lydman, and the political section chief, Edward Masters—acknowledged in interviews that they approved Mr. Martens's action in advance.

In interviews with The *New York Times*, Mr. Lydman, Mr. Masters and the two senior C.I.A. officials in Jakarta at the time of the coup denied any involvement in Mr. Martens's action.

According to the transcripts of Ms. Kadane's tape-recorded interviews, Mr. Green said he had no recollection that Mr. Martens had compiled lists of Communist Party members. Asked whether he had approved the transfer of such a list to the Indonesians, he replied, "I have no recollection of such a thing."

When Ms. Kadane said that others had confirmed it, he replied, "Well, I wouldn't gainsay it," and added, "I told you I couldn't remember it."

Role of "Top People": One Memory Fails

But the transcripts do not show conclusively that others confirmed Mr. Green's involvement. Indeed, they suggest that some embassy officials did not see the lists as sensitive or of great value to the Indonesians.

Mr. Masters at first replied, "Oh, sure," when asked if Mr. Martens told him about passing the list, the transcripts show, and he later added, "We knew where the names were going." But when asked several times if Ambassador Green or CIA officials also knew or approved, he replied: "I'm not sure anyone could remember at this late date. Let's face it, an awful lot of things were going on out there. This was not No. 1."

Mr. Masters, now head of the Washington-based National Planning Association, later told Ms. Kadane that the Indonesian military was not a group of "village idiots" and that he believed they knew how to find Communist leaders without American help.

In a final conversation with Ms. Kadane, when he became aware of what would later appear in print, Mr. Masters said: "I certainly would not disagree with the fact that we had these lists, that we were using them to check off, O.K., what was happening to the party. But the thing that is giving me trouble, and that is absolutely not correct, is that we gave these lists to the Indonesians and that they went out and picked up and killed them."

"I don't believe it," he said. "And I was in a position to know."

The transcript of an interview with Mr. Lydman includes an assertion by Ms. Kadane that "top people" in the embassy coordinated the release of the list. Mr. Lydman replied, "Oh, yes, absolutely."

But in an interview last week in Washington, where he is retired, Mr. Lydman said his response was "absolutely not what I intended."

"I certainly wasn't focusing on the impact of what she was saying," Mr. Lydman said. He said many issues were coordinated at daily staff meetings at the embassy, but that he had no knowledge of any approval for the release of the lists.

C.I.A. Involvement: Ex-Officers Speak

When interviewed for her article, the deputy C.I.A. station chief in Jakarta at the time, Joseph Lazarsky, told Ms. Kadane that the Jakarta C.I.A. station "contributed quite a bit" to Mr. Martens's lists, contradicting Mr. Martens's assertion that the lists were assembled only from press clippings.

But the C.I.A. station chief in Jakarta at the time, B. Hugh Tovar, denied that his office gave any classified information on Indonesian Communist officials to Mr. Martens.

The article also said that William Colby, a former Director of Central Intelligence who headed the C.I.A.'s Far East division in 1965, "compared the embassy's campaign to identify the P.K.I. leadership to the C.I.A.'s controversial Phoenix Program in Vietnam." Phoenix was a C.I.A.-sponsored effort to identify Communist agents within the South Vietnamese civilian population, some of whom were later killed by South Vietnamese Army units.

Mr. Colby said in a telephone interview that his remarks were "misappropriated." He noted that he had repeatedly stated publicly that the C.I.A. had no covert involvement in the Indonesian coup or its aftermath.

One observer removed from the controversy is John Hughes, a former editor of the *Christian Science Monitor* who won a Pulitzer Prize for his reporting on the Indonesian coup and later wrote a book on the subject.

Reached in Maine, where he now edits The *Camden Reporter* and The *Free Press* in nearby Rockland, Mr. Hughes said the notion that the United States Embassy would have assisted the army in locating Communists seemed "pretty far out" to him.

"I don't think the Indonesian Army needed any help in going after Communists in Indonesia at that time," he said. "It sort of boggles the mind that the embassy would need to be giving out lists. There wasn't any problem about killing people. There was an abundance of names and targets. Everybody knew who was a P.K.I. cadre."

The Massacre of the PKI Was Exaggerated

Richard Cabot Howland

Richard Cabot Howland was a foreign service officer at the US embassy in Jakarta during the period 1965–1966. In the following viewpoint, he argues that estimates of those killed during that time have been wildly exaggerated. He says that the Indonesian army was too disorganized to perform killings on a mass scale. Instead, he argues, reports of mass killings were mostly made by local officials trying to curry favor with the new regime by claiming widespread extermination of Communists. He adds that academic estimates of millions dead have been influenced by prejudice against the Indonesian regime.

"We feared the great Communist chiefs: they had magic powers which prevented them from dying. No matter how much we beat them they did not die. We had to inscribe the letters 'PKI' on their skulls to prevent their hair from growing out again after we had scalped them. Some would not die even when we forced bamboo sticks into their eyes and mouths, or after we put out their eyes. Especially in the case of the great chiefs, we would put a live cat into their bellies; only then

Richard Cabot Howland, "The Lessons of the September 30 Affair," *Studies in Intelligence* 14, Fall 1970, pp. 13–29. www.cia.gov.

would they suffocate. The cat, symbol of the tiger, caused them to lose their magic powers, and they died."

—quoted by Philippe Gavi, in an article entitled "Indonesia Days of Slaughter," in the Italian-language weekly theoretical organ of the Italian Communist Party, Rinascita (Rebirth), No. i, Rome, February 16, 1968, pp. 15–18.

Foreign estimates of the number of PKI members and sympathizers killed as a direct result of the reaction to the purge attempt have ranged from 350,000 at the low end to 1.5 million at the high. The Indonesian Government has never issued an official announcement on the subject. In a recent article in the British publication *Government and Opposition* entitled "Indonesia's Search for a Political Format," Donald Hindley quotes the low-end figure in his text but adds the latter in a footnote. Hindley is guessing, for no one really knows. His citation of both figures, an ostensible effort to attain scholarly balance, actually begs the question whether very many were killed at all. Like the "Cornell group" dissected by John T. Pizzicaro in his recent Studies in Intelligence article, Hindley is forced by the ideological compulsions of the academic "new left" to maintain the polemical attack on the New Order regime, although he personally considers it, as he once told me, "the best government Indonesia has had."

Not That Many Killed

Hindley's upper-range figure of 1.5 million was probably acquired from Miss Ruth McVey, the "PKI's biographer." Ruth was not in Indonesia at the time of the purge attempt, and had access only to journalistic sources in the months that followed. Yet by the spring of 1966, she had surfaced the figure of 1.5 million Communists dead at a New York meeting of the "Youth against War and Fascism" organization. This astonishing performance by an otherwise able and objective scholar clearly demonstrates how emotions have fogged the whole issue. How could the characteristically disorganized Indonesians possibly construct an efficient murder apparatus on this vast scale in a few months, and systematically exterminate almost one-third the number of people that the Nazi regime killed in ten years?

Following the purge attempt, Djakarta seethed with rumors and stories of bloodshed and terror. The Embassy was aware that this issue would loom large for some time and from the beginning we attempted to develop hard intelligence to put the subject in perspective. A preliminary look at the data showed, however, that even after the palpable boasts had been detected and discarded, what remained was spotty and inconsistent. No firm information on alleged killing of Communists ever emerged from almost two-thirds of Indonesia's provinces. In addition, areas where one might have expected massacres of epic proportions—diehard anti-Communist West Java, for instance—were remarkably un-stained with Communist blood. Yet in areas where the PKI had never won more than a modicum of popular support: in Atjeh, or the Madurese regions of East Java, the death tolls boggled the mind. One heard interminable lurid reports of mass killings in Bali, some 50,000 deaths or more, where the PKI had never suc-ceeded in cracking the tightly-knit Balinese social structure or challenging the political domination of the Nationalist Party. Yet in the traditional PKI stronghold of Madiun, the seat of the 1948 rebellion which should have been the first target for liquidation teams, and where there were plenty of Moslems to do the job . . . all was calm. Not one PKI death was ever reported from Madiun to my knowledge. A curious pattern, and one that did not readily hang together.

"Deliberate Misleading"

It was thus not an easy task to determine an overall death toll. Part of the problem derived from the local cultural imperative which we called "deliberate misleading of the outsider," but the Javanese call "*étok-étok*." To a Westerner, a thing is either true or false, an event either happened or it did not. This emphasis on objective reality seems dogmatic to a Javanese, who is more

Étok-Étok

I asked one informant to define *étok-étok*:

He said: "Suppose I go off south and you see me go. Later my son asks you: 'Do you know where my father went?' And you say no, *étok-étok* you don't know." I asked him why should I *étok-étok*, as there seemed to be no reason for lying, and he said, "Oh, you just *étok-étok*. You don't have to have a reason."

When we tell white lies, we have to justify them to ourselves, even though the justification [may] be weak. We tell a woman her horrible hat is pretty because it would be rude not to; if someone sees us en route to a lawyer, we may say we are going to the bank because we do not wish to advertise our troubles or have others poking into our affairs. In any case, we usually have to find some sort of reason for telling a lie. For the Javanese (especially the *prijaji*) it seems, in part anyway, to work the other way around: the burden of proof seems to be in the direction of justifying telling the truth. The natural answer to casual questions, particularly from people you do not know very well, tends to be either a vague one ("Where are you going?"—"West") or a mildly false one; and one tells the truth in small matters only when there is some reason to do so. Thus, if a Javanese is going to the movies and people ask him where he is going, he will probably tell them "to the store" unless

sensitive to the demands made on truth by the social context and his own socio-political status. Javanese seek to avoid potential conflict and embarrassment, and govern their behavior and remarks accordingly. The result is that they believe it is better to tell an outsider what they think he wishes to hear rather than risk the unpredictable consequences of telling the truth. This generalization does not pertain to all social situations, but is the cultural model for what Javanese believe social intercourse should be.

In reviewing the documentary evidence of the so-called massacre, I felt it was obvious that considerable *étok-étok* was involved. The same was true as I inquired among my contacts he wants them to join him or wants to ask them if the picture is worth seeing. When I went to see a curer with my landlord about a half-dozen people asked him along the route where he was going, and each time he replied that he was going to the house of someone a half-dozen houses or so down from where they were. It was only when he finally met someone he wished to invite to accompany him that he told the truth about his destination. In general, polite Javanese avoid gratuitous truths.

In terms of etiquette proper, *étok-étok* is especially valued as a way of concealing one's own wishes in deference to one's opposite. As one informant said: "For example, you are working. Then I come to visit. . . . I come and call out at the door. Then you act as though you were not working, not doing anything. *Étok-étok* you aren't working."

The same sort of pattern is involved in the nearly absolute requirement never to show one's real feelings directly, especially to a guest. Any kind of negative feeling toward another must be dissimulated; and people are strongly enjoined to smile and be pleasant to people for whom they have very little use. Strong positive feelings are also supposed to be hidden except in very intimate situations. The effort is to keep a steady level of very mild positive affect in interpersonal relations, an *étok-étok* warmth behind which all real feelings can be effectively concealed.

Clifford Geertz, The Religion of Java. *Chicago: University of Chicago Press, 1960, p. 246.*

in the military and elsewhere, seeking a viable nation-wide estimate of Communist deaths to report to the Department. I found an abundance of exciting, self-serving tales, told with averted eyes, as though the ghost of Aidit was lurking in the background. Rather than acting like members of a "conspiracy of silence," most people were "protesting too much" of their ruthless anti-Communist zeal. But they could not produce hard data, lists, names and places, photographs, or any indication that some Indonesian government bureau had been tasked with tracking down and collating the stories in a systematic and objective manner. It was true that Sukarno had directed several of his

Ministerial flunkies to survey Java in November 1965 to obtain information for use in his effort to stymie the anti-Communist bandwagon. But their estimate of 87,000 stemmed directly from political considerations, and had to be rejected on those grounds.

Finally, a Lieutenant Colonel in the Army's Supreme Operations Command's "Social-Political Affairs Section" passed me some figures which he swore were accurate compilations from field reporting. The totals were 50,000 dead on Java; 6,000 dead on Bali; 3,000 in North Sumatra. I was skeptical of his methods but accepted his estimates, *faute de mieux*, and combining them with my own data produced a nation-wide total of 105,000 Communists dead. Admittedly a large figure, it was still a far cry from the claims of 350,000 to 1.5 million victims being bandied about, and at least had partially resulted from a systematic effort.

While the death toll appeared lower than generally believed, the net impact on PKI cohesion and capabilities remained the same. The climate of fear and suspicion that arose in the villages as a result of the widespread rumors of mass killings effectively impaired PKI courier communications, obstructed party meetings, and thus paralyzed lateral coordination and control. Concurrently, the Army seized the central PKI publications apparatus and captured a majority of the Central Committee membership within a few months, thus blocking dissemination of instructions from the top. The PKI's two strongest features apart from identification with Sukarno, its organization and communications, were thus nullified, and its destruction as a cohesive political force was assured.

Investigation in Kediri

By April of 1966, conditions were settling down and the Army relaxed its restrictions on travel. At the first opportunity, another Embassy officer and I left on a trip through Java seeking first-hand intelligence information on a variety of subjects. Among other things, because of my conclusions mentioned above, I hoped to learn something about the alleged severe killing in East

Java which had been described in news items filed by Mr. Stanley Karnow of the St. Louis *Post-Dispatch*.

Karnow was an unusual correspondent among the many who came to Indonesia at that time. He actually visited the areas about which he wrote. He interviewed at length the Army Commander of the Kediri district of East Java, Colonel Willy Sudjono. The Colonel had filled his ears with gory details and astonishing death-tolls, including a remark that the Brantas River—which flows past Kediri town—had been "choked with 30,000 Communist bodies." From a previous trip to Kediri, I remembered the Brantas as a broad, placid stream, its bed raised above the level of the surrounding countryside by years of diking and overflow, somewhat in the manner of the Hwang Ho of China. It occurred to me that 30,000 bodies floating down the Brantas would have jammed the gates of the numerous irrigation dams that span the river, causing a severe flood in Kediri town.

In any event, I was anxious to learn just what had happened in Kediri, a fascinating area of marked importance in Javanese history and politics for centuries. It was the seat of an early Hindu-Buddhist kingdom whose legendary ruler produced a set of prophecies which became a central feature of the Javanese political mystique. Javanese believe that Kediri stands at the center of a peculiarly potent combination of necromantic and mystical geo-magnetic forces. The area in consequence has generated peasant-based millenarian movements for hundreds of years. Prince Diponegoro of Jogjakarta went to Kediri to meditate in a cave before he fomented a messianic revolt against the Dutch in 1821. Sukarno always played up his early boyhood in Blitar, near Kediri, and had requested to be interred there. Before the 1965 purge attempt, Kediri was a Sukarnoist/PKI stronghold, as one might expect where severe ethnic (Javanese vs. Madurese) and religious (reformist Moslem vs. animist) antagonisms intersected in a setting that contrasted large land-holdings with abysmal poverty. Here were all the contradictions which provided, for Sukarno and the PKI, the exploitable corridors of power.

In April 1966, another Embassy officer and myself spent several days at the home of an American Baptist missionary doctor and his wife in Kediri. The Baptist mission and hospital were established in Kediri just after the war. They were readily accepted by the nominal Moslem Javanese of the area, who probably saw the Baptists as just another mystical sect drawn to Kediri by its potent ethereal forces. There were eight American families and many "national preachers"—local converts who helped spread the gospel—at the Baptist establishment. They enjoyed excellent relations with local officials and had made many friends in the villages of the area. Every morning, Javanese from all social classes lined up in front of the hospital for medical treatment. Obviously the Baptists were well-attuned to the local environment.

From several days' talks with the Baptist group and other local informants, an interesting picture of Colonel Willy Sudjono emerged. He had lost several relatives fighting on the Communist side at Madiun in 1948. He was also known as a staunch Sukarnoist and devout follower of the pro-Communist East Java mystical sect leader, Mbah Suro. Before the purge attempt, he had not obstructed the Communist advance. The missionaries remarked that during the August 17, 1965, National Day celebrations, PKI organizations marched down Kediri's main street for hours, some of them armed, while Willy Sudjono watched and smiled. Yet the missionaries did not believe he was a Communist himself. They had requested troops to protect the hospital against threatened PKI attacks on several occasions, and he had always complied. Sudjono's family came to the hospital for medical treatment and health exams, as did many of the local officials of the area. Obviously there was more to his story than Karnow had learned.

No Sign of Slaughter
The missionaries and their local contacts had heard many stories of mass killings in the surrounding area, including the tale of "30,000 bodies choking the Brantas River." One night, accord-

ing to a missionary wife, they heard the *gamelans* (traditional musical instruments) "pounding from darkness till dawn." They presumed that killing was underway, and that the music was intended to cover the sound of screams. They were surprised that fanatical Moslems would choose to kill by *gamelan* music, a non-Moslem, Hindu-Javanese cultural manifestation. But the next morning, everything was calm. As the Baptists went through nearby villages, there was no sign of slaughter. In fact, although they preached and dispensed health care in the area throughout the period of the purge attempt and its aftermath, none ever saw a Communist body, in the Brantas or elsewhere. Whenever they asked village contacts about the subject, they were always told that "there were no PKI members in this village and no killing here, but many dead at the next village down the road." But at the next village, the answer was the same: "no PKI, no killing here."

A press correspondent who spent a month on Bali searching for evidence of the mass killings for a feature story told me that he had gotten the same answer in village after village there. Moreover, he pointed out, neither he nor his colleagues had ever managed to photograph a Communist body. To this day, I myself have never seen even one photograph of a PKI corpse.

The missionaries' story was confirmed by other local informants, who believed that most of the Communist leaders had fled to Surabaja after the failure of the purge attempt, while the peasant masses who had supported the party because of its identification with Sukarno simply melted away. What killing had occurred, they said, had been on a minor, ceremonial scale.

Thus, there must have been considerable *étok-étok* in the story Willy Sudjono told Stan Karnow. He had done nothing to slow down the PKI in his jurisdiction before the purge attempt. As a known Sukarnophile and Mbah Suro devotee, the onus was on him afterwards to demonstrate his loyalty to the Army. He must have welcomed the chance to proclaim to Djakarta through an American journalist that his severity toward the party after the event had known no bounds.

Inflating Numbers

How many other local military commanders and district officials had been under the same pressures after the purge attempt?
Virtually all of them were imbued with Sukarno's "Nasakom" slo-
ganry, including the policy of collaborating with the PKI. What
better way to display their newly-discovered anti-Communist
colors, without committing themselves to Suharto or Sukarno
while the Djakarta power struggle was unresolved, than by inflat-
ing the numbers of PKI killed in their jurisdictions? How many
opportunistic politicians sought to erase years of riding the PKI's
coat-tails by proclaiming responsibility for a few unverifiable
Communist deaths? The IP-KI Party leader Lucas Kustarjo, for
instance, though a long-time Sukarnophile, boasted everywhere
that he had told Sukarno personally that he killed "300 PKI leaders with his own hands."

Like the politicians and military leaders, the average village
citizen had shrewd motivations for concocting massacre tales.
If a villager told the authorities that his Communist neighbor
had escaped, he risked guilt by association, or at least faced
the prospect of a harangue on the importance of "heightening
vigilance against the PKI." But if he told the authorities that his
Communist neighbor had been killed by the "spontaneity of the
masses," he would receive a pat on the back—perhaps even his
neighbor's house or land. Who could check the story? The Army
has never been able to keep track of its own personnel, let alone
the civilians on over-populated Java.

As the reports of massacres moved up along the chain of
command, they could easily have been embellished and mag-
nified as successive layers of officialdom sought to display their
own anti-Communist zeal. The natural tendency was to accept
them at face value, especially among the Western correspon-
dents who flocked to Djakarta in search of sensational copy for
lurid feature articles to cable to the outside world. The result was
the myth of the massacre. A good part of it must have been *étok-
étok* by everyone concerned.

The 1965 Killings Constituted Genocide

Robert Cribb

Robert Cribb is a professor of history at the Australian National University. In the following viewpoint, he argues that the killings in Indonesia were widespread and systematic and were intended to eradicate Communists and their influence in Indonesia. He says, moreover, that Communists were treated as an ethnic group, with their children facing discrimination and stigma for generations after the killings. Since national identity was seen as so central to Indonesian identity, and since Communists were seen as embodying a particular vision of Indonesian identity, Cribb argues that the mass killing of Communists was similar in many respects to genocidal slayings of ethnic groups. He concludes that the 1965–1966 killings were genocide.

Early in the morning of October 1, 1965, [an] atmosphere of enormous tension and expectation was shattered by what appeared to be a communist coup in Jakarta. Left-wing troops raided the houses of seven leading anti-communist generals, including the army commander General Ahmad Yarn and the defence minister General A.H. Nasution. Three were shot on the spot and three were hauled off to an air force base south of Jakarta where they were killed. Nasution escaped under fire, but his young daughter was killed. The leader of the action was Lieutenant–Colonel Untung, commander of Sukarno's presidential guard. After a brief delay, he declared that he had acted to forestall a military coup by an alleged "Council of General" and that state power was now in the hands of a Revolutionary Council. Whether or not the plotters had originally intended to kill the generals, their actions after dawn on October 1 showed little sign of careful planning. The Revolutionary Council appeared to have been composed in haste, without any attempt to consult those named as members, and the plotters did not take serious measures to seize the important points of control in Jakarta or to neutralize potential opponents. As a result, forces from the army's Strategic Reserve, headed by Lieutenant–General Suharto, were able to take the initiative and to put an end to the "coup" within a couple of days.

The Coup and Its Aftermath

The nature of the "coup" remains uncertain. It may have been the initiative of junior army officers unhappy with the lifestyles and political conservatism of the High Command and was perhaps intended to do no more than humiliate and intimidate the senior officers. If so, the action got badly out of hand. On the other hand, the junior officers may themselves have had more far-reaching intentions, or they may have been the dupes of other political forces with broader intentions. Both the Communist Party and President Sukarno had good reason to want the removal of the army High Command. Indeed, it is unlikely that the junior officers would have taken action against their superiors in the military hierarchy unless they felt sure of some political protection. Whether they assumed they would get such protection or were promised it remains uncertain. It is known that a special bureau of the Communist Party was in routine contact with some of the coup plotters as part of the party's general aim of winning support in the ranks of its most powerful opponent. Also possible is that the coup was to some extent prompted or planned by enemies of Sukarno and the communists in order to compromise them. There is inconclusive but not entirely negligible evidence implicating both Suharto and the American Central Intelligence Agency in this respect.

Whoever may have been responsible for the "coup," however, most Indonesians and most outside observers assumed at once that it was the work of the Communist Party. Indeed, many members of the party seem to have made the same assumption: if the coup were a party initiative, it could hardly have been announced in advance to the three million members scattered across the country. Still more important, most Indonesians interpreted the evident failure of the "coup" as a profound defeat for the party. In the hothouse world of Guided Democracy [the Indonesian political system under Sukarno] the communists seemed to have a chance of coming to power by dominating discourse and annexing the important instruments of government. When the killing of the generals failed to cement an immediate communist seizure of power, everyone knew that the party's chances of taking power in the short term had disappeared. The tense balance of Guided Democracy was shattered and the army would not permit the communists to come to power. The party and its three million members were suddenly helpless.

The Demonization of the Communists

Still more seriously for the communists, their opponents were able to exploit the circumstances of the "coup" to demonize them. To begin with, murdered generals were Indonesia's first significant victims of political assassination since the chaos of the revolution against the Dutch in the 1940s. In resorting to such violence the plotters had taken the tense confrontations of Indonesian politics to another level of bitterness. The killing of Nasution's daughter, moreover, marked communists as conscienceless child-killers, even though it had clearly been accidental. The real vilification of the party, however, began with the exhumation of the bodies of the murdered generals. Wild stories began to be circulated of the events at the air force base: members of the women's organization Gerwani, generally seen as a communist affiliate, were said to have tortured and mutilated the generals sexually before abandoning themselves in a lustful orgy with senior communists and air force officers. Before long, rumours began to circulate that party members had prepared pits—cunningly disguised as rubbish pits—to receive the bodies of their slain enemies. Newspapers published accounts, sometimes graphically illustrated, of how communists had been trained to turn simple implements such as rubber-tapping implements into gruesome eye-gouging tools. This demonization of the communists in turn made it easier for people to believe that the party was the prime cause of Indonesia's economic malaise, that the communists had deliberately created hardship and suffering to serve their own political ends. In a matter of weeks, by skilful exploitation of rumour and propaganda in an environment of enormous uncertainty and tension, the opponents of the Communist Party were able to turn it from being a recognized, if somewhat feared, element in the Indonesian political system into a pariah.

The Killings

The massacre of communists began in early October in the strongly Muslim province of Aceh in northern Sumatra. The local branch of the party was small, the initiative for the killings seems to have come from local Muslim leaders, and Acehnese Muslims had a long-standing reputation for using violence against their enemies. Elsewhere, there was a longer delay, as both sides assessed the situation. In most cases, the killings were triggered by the arrival of anti-communist special forces, especially the RPKAD para-commandos, or when local armed forces made it clear that they sanctioned the murder of communists. In some regions, military units themselves took a major role in the killing, but more commonly they used local militias. All of Indonesia's political parties had youth affiliates whose activities shaded into intimidation, protection and small-scale violence, but the army, jealous of its monopoly of armed force, had never permitted them to develop beyond a limited scale. In the aftermath of the 1965 "coup," however, the military began to provide weapons, equipment, training and encouragement to these youth organizations, especially the Muslim Ansor in Central and East Java. These organizations typically moved systematically from village to village using lists and local informants to identify party members, who were then taken away for execution. In some cases, entire villages were wiped out, but for the most part, the killers were selective, taking only those that were identified as "guilty." Teachers and other village intellectuals were especially common on the lists of victims. The killing was largely done with knives or swords, but some victims were beaten to death and some were shot. Sometimes the bodies of the victims were deliberately mutilated, an act which, for Muslims, damages the spiritual integrity of the victim's soul. In some cases, the victims were forced to dig their own shallow, mass graves in secluded places, or the bodies were dumped in rivers, or concealed in caves. There are some reports of mass graves beneath the main square in towns in central Java. In a few cases, the bodies, or body parts, of victims were put on display, sometimes laid out on rafts, which were floated down rivers.

The regions most seriously affected by the killings were Central and East Java, Bali and North Sumatra, where the party had been most active, but there were massacres in every part of the archipelago where communists could be found. No reliable figures exist for the number of people who were killed. A scholarly consensus has settled on a figure of 400–500,000, but the correct figure could be half or twice as much. Indonesia had a population at the time between 100 and 110 million, too many for even a million deaths to show up incontrovertibly in the decennial censuses. Although official figures seem to have been

Indonesian Nationalist youths bearing bamboo spears and hatchets accompany Indonesian Army patrol around Mount Merapi, Java, to search for the Communist leader D.N. Aidit and his followers in 1965. © Bettmann/Corbis/AP Photo.

compiled in many regions, there are many reasons why figures might have been over- or understated by those responsible for their collection.

As in many cases of genocide, many of the victims went passively to their deaths. There are reports that victims in one place in the province of North Sumatra formed long, acquiescent lines at a river's edge while they waited to be decapitated. In Bali, party members are said to have gone placidly to their deaths wearing traditional white funeral clothes. In parts of central Java, predominantly communist villages set up palisades in a futile attempt at self-defence, but even such measures were rare. One reason for the apparent passivity of the victims may be that they simply did not expect such ferocious retaliation for events in Jakarta to which they could not possibly have contributed. It is likely, however, that the explanation is partly cultural-historical: for most of human history, Indonesia has been relatively sparsely populated, a consequence of tropical disease and, possibly, of the relatively high standing of women, whose role in society was always far more than just the production of children. Wars of conquest in early times, therefore, generally aimed at capturing people, rather than territory. Battle by proxy or champion— a way of minimizing casualties—was reasonably common and there was no tradition of wholesale massacre such as was found, for instance, in densely populated China. Peoples, however, still had to be conquered, and conquered peoples had to be ruled; an important part of the political repertoire of conquerors and rulers, therefore, came to be intimidation. A cultural convention arose in which the correct and safe response to fearsomeness was timidity: those who showed themselves suitably in awe of new power-holders were spared. This cultural convention probably sapped the will of the communists to resist in 1965–1966.

Silence About the Killings

Remarkably little primary evidence exists concerning the detail of the killings. The military-dominated regime of President Suharto, which had presided over the killings and which ruled Indonesia for more than 30 years afterwards, strongly discouraged any investigation of the events, though it has never denied that they took place. Indeed, the nearest thing to an official estimate of the number of dead is one million. The fact that the killings took place, moreover, at the height of the Cold War meant that there was little interest in the West in investigating the past misdeeds of what was to become one of the West's most important allies in Asia. As a result, several misconceptions about the nature of the killings have become common. Some observers, for instance, have suggested that many of the killings were apolitical, that people took advantage of the turmoil to settle private grudges unrelated to politics. The reality was, however, that the Communist Party had been so successful in taking sides in social conflicts across the breadth of the archipelago that most grudges had a political dimension. All the evidence that we have indicates that the killings were precisely directed against the broad category of people whom the army identified as enemies, that is, the members and close associates of the Communist Party. Also sometimes heard is the suggestion that the killings were a form of "running amok" (*amok* being after all an Indonesian word). It was argued that traditional Indonesian (especially Javanese) peasant society was inherently peaceful, but that under conditions of extreme tension that natural patience of the Javanese suddenly shattered in a blind frenzy of killing. Apart from overstating the peacefulness of traditional Indonesian society, however, this argument has the weakness that [the killings] were highly targeted. Furthermore, psycho-cultural studies of *amok* have shown that it is most commonly a response to humiliation and defeat and often works as a form of indirect suicide. Little in the detail of the 1965–1966 killings fits with this pattern.

Also surprisingly common is the perception that most of the victims were Chinese. For the reasons outlined above, Chinese Indonesians have been subject to discrimination, harassment and occasional pogroms for at least the last 250 years. In 1965–1966, however, few Chinese were targeted. This was partly because discriminatory measures a few years earlier had removed most Chinese from the countryside where the vast majority of killings took place, partly because Chinese, as outsiders, were not immediately involved in the massive resolution of issues which was taking place. "They [the Chinese] were not involved," commented a non-communist leader years later, "it was a matter between Javanese."

Army or Local Initiative?

Perhaps the most intractable difficulty, however, lies in determining the relative importance of army initiative and local tension in accounting for the scale of the killing. At first glance, the army's role seems clearly secondary to that of the broader social and political tensions outlined above. The hatred between Islamists and communists was ancient and deep-seated and had been exacerbated by the deep political uncertainty and enormous political tension of late Guided Democracy. The army, on the other hand, had the luxury of knowing that it had won: the failure of the October, 1965 "coup" meant that the Communist Party would not come to power under Guided Democracy. Imprisonment or execution of a few thousand leading communists would have been ample to guarantee the army's victory. The commander of the RPKAD was widely reported at the time as claiming that his troops had sought to curb the killings in Bali.

Nonetheless, several factors point to a greater direct military role. As we have seen, the killings tended to take place when anti-communist army units arrived in a region, and the militias who did much of the killing received weapons, equipment, training and encouragement from the army. More significant, the militias seem to have vanished as soon as their bloody work was done. The autonomous militias which had emerged after 1945 to fight for independence against the Dutch proved to be a stubborn and persistent obstacle to the army's claim to a monopoly of armed force and one of the most important lessons which the army learnt from this period was not to allow that monopoly to be breached. Even during the early 1980s, the military had to resort to extensive violence to suppress semi-criminal gangs who had been used as paramilitary enforcers in the larger cities. The rapid and peaceful disappearance of militias who were ostensibly linked to Muslim forces suspicious of the army's developmentalism strongly suggests that they were in fact creations of the military.

If the army did indeed want a full-scale massacre of communists, three reasons seem plausible. First, although we can see in retrospect that the army's victory was sealed by the failure of the October, 1965 "coup," this fact was by no means clear at the time. In particular, the army was aware of a kind of "shadow war" with the communists which involved placing sympathizers, agents and double-agents in key positions. The army did not know just how far the communist penetration of society and of government institutions had proceeded, and it therefore made certain of delivering the party a death-blow by killing a vast number of its followers. In this atmosphere of suspicion, moreover, people who feared that they might be identified as communists often took part in killings to prove their anti-communist credentials. As mass killings, too—killings by masses as well as of them— the massacres also had the purpose of forcing all Indonesians to make an unambiguous choice for or against the Communist Party. Just in case the communists were to recover and mount a counter-offensive, the military needed to be sure that blood was on as many hands as possible. Thus there are many stories of forcible recruitment into the militias and even of family members being forced to take the first step in killing their relatives. Communists from one village were sometimes delivered to another for killing, and the whole village was thus implicated in the murders, regardless of which hands actually held the murder weapons. The hesitant fence-sitters of Guided Democracy who had done everything possible to make sure that they would survive, whoever came to power, were to have that luxury no longer. This strategy still works: when Indonesia's new president, Abdurrachman Wahid, recently suggested that an inquiry be made into the massacres of 1965–1966, an inquiry which would certainly have added to the opprobrium currently being heaped on the armed forces, Muslim leaders from his own party moved very quickly to prevent the inquiry from going ahead. Youth groups from this party had been active in the killings in many parts of Java. Third, whether or not it was intended at the time, the killings hugely reinforced the army's political position once it was in power. For those who recognized the military role in the killings, the army was a force which had shown its willingness to kill on a vast scale, and it gave no reason to doubt that it would do so again if action seemed to be needed. For those who saw the killings as a product of internecine strife between rival Indonesians, military rule, whatever its shortcomings, seemed to be a guarantee against a repetition of that terrible time. The massacres placed a curse on open politics, which was not lifted for more than three decades.

Hereditary Communism

A final likely reason why the army wanted the mass killings brings the genocide in Indonesia still closer to the ethnic genocides, which dominate traditional analysis of the term. Even after the killings subsided, the army appeared to show an especial vindictiveness towards communists. During the 10 years which followed the killings, over a million and a half people passed through a system of prisons and prison camps on the grounds of their communist connections. When they were finally released, their lives were blighted by continuing discrimination, they were banned from government jobs, they were not permitted to vote and they faced difficulties in day-to-day dealings with the authorities. In the late 1980s, the authorities introduced a new concept, *bersih lingkungan* ("environmentally clean"), under which government employees and workers in education, the media and law, as well as economically important sectors such as the oil industry and public transportation, were expected to come from a family and social environment untainted by communism. In other words, communism was treated as a permanent, semi-hereditary condition which might afflict even people born after 1965.

All these generalizations must be read, however, in the light of the enormous variation in circumstances from province to province across Indonesia and from district to district within provinces. The few local studies to have been published show a complex interaction between long-standing local political tensions, varying responses to events in Jakarta, and different personalities in local institutions. In some districts the killing was truly collective; in others the military did most of the killing; in still others local men of violence emerged to glut themselves on slaughter.

The Suharto regime was not Stalin's Soviet Union or even Hitler's Germany after 1943. The so-called New Order did not feed on a widening circle of terror, sucking innocent and guilty alike into graves and gulags for the sake of terrifying effect. It was brutal in its treatment of enemies, real and presumed, and sometimes erratic in identifying them, but the last pogroms against communists were in 1969. Thereafter the only communists to die at the hands of the state were an unfortunate handful who had been sentenced to death in show trials in the late 1960s and from whom the government occasionally picked a few victims for execution.

But the Indonesian killings of 1965–1966 were a successful exercise in national obliteration. They were a concerted attempt to transform the nature of Indonesian society by destroying one of the three ideological and social streams [nationalism, Islam, and communism] which had competed for domination of the idea of Indonesia since the early twentieth century. We should not suppose that the communists would necessarily have been less brutal or that they would have ruled better if they had come to power rather than the army. But the killing of half a million communists was not merely an intense political conflict, it was the impoverishment of a national ideal, the extermination of a nation as it has existed in the minds of millions of Indonesians.

Suharto Was a Thoughtful and Effective Leader, Despite Flaws

Richard Woolcott

Richard Woolcott is an Australian diplomat who worked extensively with Indonesia's President Suharto. In the following viewpoint, written on the occasion of Suharto's death, he presents Suharto as a thoughtful and talented leader who maintained security and peace in Indonesia for decades. He acknowledges that Suharto's regime had problems, including corruption and human rights violations, but argues that these have been exaggerated. He says that history will judge Suharto kindly. Woolcott makes no mention of the 1965–1966 genocide in his evaluation.

The death of Suharto in Jakarta last night, at the age of 86, will give rise to different evaluations of his contribution to Indonesia, to the Southeast Asian region and to Australian-Indonesian relations.

I first met Suharto when I visited Indonesia with prime minister William McMahon in 1972. I last met him in 1997 as chairman of the Australia-Indonesia Institute.

Richard Woolcott, "Suharto as I Knew Him," *The Australian*, January 28, 2008. Copyright © 2008 by The Australian. All rights reserved. Reproduced by permission.

In the intervening quarter of a century I had the opportunity over numerous meetings to assess the man, his leadership qualities and his contribution to his country and to our shared neighbourhood.

Tough as Old Boots

I always found Suharto polite and congenial. While cautious about expressing views until he had reflected on a situation and shaped them in his own mind, and regarded by many as taciturn, I found that once he knew you, he was friendly, relaxed and willing to listen. He also articulated his own views clearly, especially his vision for Indonesia.

In conversations he smiled frequently. In fact he was known in Merdeka Palace circles as the "smiling general".

Behind that engaging smile there was, however, a firm resolve. Paul Keating once said to him at a meeting on November 15, 1997, that he had told some other APEC [Asia-Pacific Economic Cooperation] leaders that he, Suharto, "was as tough as old boots". He was. He stood by his friends and stuck firmly to his views once they were formed.

Suharto was not an intellectual but he was shrewd and knew what he did not know. Knowing little about an economy that was in chaos in 1965, he chose civilian Berkeley University-educated economists (widely known as the Berkeley Mafia) to rescue the economy. These key economic ministers included Professor Widjojo, Ali Wardhana, Professor Sadli and Emil Salim.

Suharto was also reliable. If he said he would do something, it would be carried out. As Singapore's former prime minister and present minister mentor Lee Kuan Yew described him, Suharto was "a man of his word". Lee also recognised the major contribution Suharto made to regional stability in Southeast Asia during the 1970s and 80s.

Suharto, like most Javanese, played his cards close to his chest. I recall once having a private discussion with the governor of Central Java, Soepardjo, who had become a good friend. It was shortly before the 1996 presidential election. I asked Soepardjo who he thought was most likely to be nominated by Suharto as his vice-president. I always remember his reply.

"Dick," he said, "as you know, the president and I have been comrades in arms. I have been a trusted friend for many years. I am the governor of the president's province, the most populous province in Indonesia, Central Java. I spent an hour with the Bapak yesterday. It was an empat mata (four eyes only) meeting. We discussed the current state of politics. Yet I left that meeting with no idea who he might nominate in just a few days' time. I know him as well as anybody but I could read nothing in his expression."

Often Misunderstood

It is hardly surprising that Suharto was sometimes misunderstood by Australian leaders.

In January 1976 I accompanied foreign minister Andrew Peacock on a call on the president. Peacock said he wanted to raise with Suharto the possibility of a UN force in East Timor following Indonesia's invasion the previous month.

I advised him against doing so on the grounds that it would not be prudent to present an important new idea to the president without some prior notification, preferably through his colleague, the Indonesian foreign minister. Peacock ignored this advice as, of course, he was entitled to do and towards the end of the conversation he made this proposal to the president. Suharto's face was an impassive mask. When Peacock finished, he simply nodded.

In the car after the call, Peacock said: "You see, he agreed."

"No," I replied. "Suharto's nod was not a nod indicating assent. It was a Javanese nod, which simply means I have heard what you have said." A few days later, the proposal for a UN force was officially rejected.

Probably because of his army training, Suharto was somewhat hierarchical and conscious of status. For example, he declined, as head of state of Indonesia, to receive Sir Ninian Stephen when he

Australia and Indonesia

Condemned by geography to be neighbors, there are no two countries that have been more asymmetrically disparate, different, and thus distant as are Australia and Indonesia. This has been aptly described by a number of political observers. Gareth Evans, the former Australian foreign minister, argued, "no two neighbors anywhere in the world are as comprehensively unlike as Australia and Indonesia. We differ in language, culture, religion, history, ethnicity, population size and in political, legal and social systems." Professor Desmond Ball, coeditor of *Strange Neighbors: The Australian-Indonesian Relationship,* similarly argued that "although the fact of geography has placed us next door to each other, we are in many significant respects strangers. We share many common interests, including the objectives of a stable and secure region and economic well-being. But we also have many differences. We are quite unlike

wanted to visit Indonesia in 1986. Suharto acknowledged Queen Elizabeth II as Australia's head of state, not the governor-general. In Suharto's eyes, Sir Ninian was her representative.

Suharto, like many Javanese, was attracted to mysticism. One of his confidants and spiritual advisers was Sudjono Humardani. Before taking a major decision Suharto would often meditate with Sudjono, occasionally at a special cave on the Dieng Plateau to which, incidentally, he took Gough Whitlam in a rare gesture in 1974.

Exaggerated Criticism

Strident criticism, especially from the political Left, of Suharto as a brutal, corrupt military dictator ruling an expansionist Indonesia has always been exaggerated.

Suharto was certainly authoritarian and relied on the armed forces for support. He was also pragmatic, secular and opposed to Islamic extremism. I was surprised to find when I arrived in in our respective cultural heritages, religious beliefs and practices, political structures, demographic bases, levels and patterns of economic development and military forces and defense policies." In the same vein, a leading Indonesian strategic thinker, Lieutenant-General Hasnan Habib, argued that "relations between Indonesia and Australia have never been close or very friendly, the principal reason being the latter's distrust of the former, which is perceived as a threat. This attitude had its roots in both nations' great differences of philosophy, history, culture, value systems and geography. This distrust is often manifested in annoyingly arrogant, condescending, self-righteous, and rude comments on various issues of Indonesia's domestic affairs, which disregard Indonesia's feelings and sensitivities."

Bilveer Singh, Defense Relations Between Australia and Indonesia in the Post-Cold War Era. *Westport, CT: Greenwood, 2002, p. 19.*

Jakarta as our ambassador in 1975 that there were a disproportionate five Christians in the cabinet.

On a farewell call shortly before my return to Australia in 1978, Suharto asked me to remind Australian ministers that the threat to his government and to Indonesia's stability came not from any recrudescence of the Indonesian Communist Party but from Islamic fundamentalism, especially if it were to secure external support.

One of Suharto's main contributions to Indonesian stability was in fact to maintain religious tolerance which has, regrettably, broken down since he was ousted.

Far from being expansionist, the whole thrust of Suharto's foreign policy after 1966 was to regain the confidence of the West and of his neighbours, especially Singapore and Malaysia, following Sukarno's erratic anti-Western policy and his Konfrontasi [policy of confrontation] against the establishment of Malaysia.

He saw Indonesia as the successor state to Dutch colonial possessions in Southeast Asia. Indonesia had always acknowledged Portuguese sovereignty over East Timor.

It was only after the breakdown of Portuguese decolonisation policy in 1974–75 and when the prospect emerged of a left wing, independent but aid-dependent mini-state within the Indonesian archipelago, at the height of the Cold War, that he agreed to his military advisers' firm recommendations that the colony must be incorporated, if necessary by force.

In the light of the civil war that had erupted and Portugal's abandonment of its colony in 1975, he first authorised covert Indonesian involvement and then the invasion on December 6. His motivation was not territorial expansion. It was national security. In other circumstances his clear preference was for the peaceful political integration of East Timor when it was decolonised.

In 1964, when I visited Indonesia from Singapore, where I was Australian commissioner, I could sense the coming social explosion that brought the then little known Major General Suharto to power. At that time, 70 per cent of Indonesia's population lived below the UN poverty line. Per capita income was only $US74. Less than 50 per cent of primary school-aged children were in school.

Thirty years later, those living below the poverty line had been reduced to 14 per cent. Per capita income had risen to $US997 (a more than 13-fold increase) and a large middle class had developed. Ninety-six per cent of primary school-aged children were in school. World Bank projections in 1995 (since overtaken by the unpredicted East Asian financial crisis in 1997) suggested Indonesia would be the world's fifth-largest economy by 2020.

Indonesia's stability and economic progress between 1975 and 1995 were indeed remarkable. No other developing country achieved comparable progress. Much of the credit for this transformation should be given to Suharto and his key civilian economic ministers. At the same time Indonesia had translated its progress into increased regional and international stature.

The Dark Side of Suharto

There was, of course, the dark side to his long presidency. Suharto demonstrated four principal flaws. First, he identified Indonesia's progress and stability with his own continuing leadership. He stayed too long. Had he stepped down in 1992 or even in 1997, history would, I believe, record his presidency more favourably than it now might. But he made no proper arrangements for an orderly succession, such as Tunku Abdul Rahman had made in Malaysia and Lee in Singapore.

Second, he was unresponsive to concerns about human rights. He acquiesced in the removal of those who stood in the way of what he considered was best for Indonesia or who were publicly opposed to his policies.

He also tolerated abuses of human rights by the armed forces, especially in East Timor, Aceh and Papua.

Third, he abandoned his earlier policy of gradual political liberalisation in favour of trying to consolidate his own power. This inhibited his ability to respond to legitimate popular aspirations and to manage growing pressures for change, especially in the 90s.

Suharto was not by nature a democrat. He saw democracy, especially in a developing country, as divisive and wasteful of talent. He had seen the first attempt fail under Sukarno. He believed that at Indonesia's stage of development the most appropriate form of government for a country of such size and diversity was a strong centralised administration. Otherwise national unity could not be maintained.

Democracy only worked, and even then not always efficiently, in Western societies with generally high levels of prosperity and education. He did not regard Indian democracy as likely to prove effective.

History is therefore likely to record that one of Suharto's major failures was that he did not nourish the institutions Indonesia would need in the future: namely an independent judiciary, a free press and, especially, representative political institutions. In fact, he undermined and prevented the evolution along these lines of the judiciary, the media and the parliament. When the economic crisis struck in 1997 and the political crisis in 1998, Indonesian institutions were too fragile to cope, a situation that prevails to this day and for which Suharto must take most of the responsibility.

Fourth, corruption, cronyism and nepotism increased substantially in the latter stages of his presidency.

In particular, he permitted his children to enrich themselves grossly by intruding into virtually all lucrative contracts and monopolies. This situation worsened after the death of his wife, Ibu Tien, in April 1996. A degree of restraint probably departed with her.

Indonesia and Australia

Turning to bilateral relations, Suharto was genuinely interested in Australia. I returned with him for his last visit for informal talks in Townsville in April 1975 with Whitlam. Suharto's positive approach to trade liberalisation and to Asia-Pacific economic co-operation was to be of great value to Australia.

When I called on him in April 1989 as Bob Hawke's special envoy to advance the idea of an Asia-Pacific Economic Co-operation forum, he was cautious but supportive. His subsequent support was critical in securing the agreement of the other ASEAN [Association of Southeast Asian Nations] countries to this major Australian initiative.

Later, in November 1994, as the host for the APEC leaders' meeting in Bogor, encouraged by prime minister Keating, Suharto again showed decisive leadership, as the president of one of the world's major developing countries, in committing Indonesia—and because of its influence—the other countries of Southeast Asia to the free trade agenda embodied in the Bogor Declaration and to a more open international trading system.

The Agreement on Mutual Security signed on December 18, 1995, was another area in which Suharto showed leadership in a way that was helpful to Australia and to regional security. It was a confidence-building measure and demonstrated to both the Australian and Indonesian communities that we had a shared interest in the security of our region. It was an important evolution of Hawke's belief that Australia must find its security "with and not against Indonesia".

It is a matter for regret that due to the mutual mishandling in Jakarta and Canberra of aspects of Timor policy in 1999, prime minister John Howard chose to describe the AMS [Australian-Indonesian Agreement on Maintaining Security] as "irrelevant", which led regrettably to its abrogation by an angry president BJ Habibie. This is an unfortunate episode because, both in Opposition in 1995 and later in office, the Howard government had strongly supported this agreement. It has since been replaced by a new agreement drafted by the Howard government.

Suharto's presidency spanned nine Australian prime ministers, from Robert Menzies to Howard. In November 1975, I conveyed a personal message from Malcolm Fraser as caretaker prime minister to Suharto, stating that if elected he wished to develop the same close personal relationship with Suharto that Whitlam had built up. Suharto had a sense of humour and while he welcomed Fraser's attitude, he commented with a wry smile: "Many people in your country think of Indonesia as unstable. Malcolm Fraser will be the sixth Australian prime minister with whom I have dealt!"

Managing a chain of 13,600 islands, stretching the distance from Broome in Western Australia to Christchurch in New Zealand, with a population of about 230 million people composed of about 300 ethnic groups and speaking about 250 distinct languages, is by any standard a massive political challenge. It is one of the reasons why Australian prime ministers from Holt to Howard were impressed by Suharto's leadership.

I suspect that although there were important flaws in his presidency, Suharto's 32-year rule will be judged more objectively by future historians than it is likely to be now, especially in Australia.

Suharto Was a Corrupt Tyrant Who Damaged Indonesia

John Gittings

John Gittings is a journalist, formerly of The Guardian, *and the author of* The Changing Face of China: From Mao to Market. *In the following viewpoint, written on the death of Suharto, he argues that the dictator was brutal, corrupt, and ultimately ineffective. He discusses Suharto's role in the 1965 genocide, and says he kept control of Indonesia throughout his regime through repression and clever manipulation of the military elite. Gittings says that the West supported Suharto, including his brutal actions in East Timor, because of his anti-communism thrust. Eventually, Gittings concludes, Suharto's corruption and half-baked economic schemes caught up with him, leaving Indonesia weakened in the face of the 1997 Asian economic crisis, and finally driving Suharto from power.*

The death of the former Indonesian president Suharto at the age of 86 reminds us that even the most stubborn of dictatorships come to an end. Despite predictions by his ruling clique that he would lead Indonesia into the 21st century, his term of office, which began with bloodshed in 1967, ended equally bloodily in 1998. Although known as the "smiling general", he had a complex character which, for most of his life, successfully deflected analysis. He was acclaimed as a man of modest origins who had taken power out of disgust at the corruption of the last years of Sukarno, Indonesia's first president, who ruled from its independence from the Netherlands in 1949 until 1967.

Bloody Beginning, Bloody End

For years, this myth coexisted with the public knowledge that Suharto presided over a regime in which his closest friends controlled huge monopolies and lucrative concessions, while his children acquired assets worth billions of dollars.

Under his rule, Indonesia became closely aligned with western interests during the cold war and was rewarded with aid and investment to foster rapid economic growth, making fortunes for his cronies. He favoured ambitious, but often unsound, development projects, and schemes to relocate millions of landless peasants and open up virgin forests paved the way for the country's current environmental crisis.

Vast numbers of political opponents were killed, jailed or sent to labour camps during three decades of Suharto's rule, with tens of thousands dying in East Timor alone following its illegal annexation in 1975.

Suharto lost his grip on power only when the Asian financial crisis of 1997 led to popular unrest over rocketing prices and unemployment, to which he had no answer except repression.

His political career ended in May 1998, two months after he had insisted on standing for a seventh presidential term and appointed a cabinet dominated by his old friends and family. The killing of six students by security forces at Trisakti University on May 12 triggered a revulsion to which even Suharto had to yield.

It was grimly fitting that a regime that began in blood with the slaughter of hundreds of thousands in an anti-communist crackdown from 1965 to 1966 ended with more bloodshed. Only then could the Suharto myth begin to be unravelled.

Early Years

It had been a long journey from his birthplace, the village of Godean, around 25 miles from Jogjakarta, the former royal capital in central Java.

His father was a minor official under Dutch rule, supervising water distribution to the fields, in return for which he was allocated two acres to farm. His mother had distant aristocratic origins, being descended from one of the sultan of Jogjakarta's concubines some generations back. Suharto himself seems to have been rather unhappy, and frequently changed his name through life—a Javanese device to fend off evil spirits at a time of personal failure.

His parents separated when he was small, and he then lived with relatives. He spent some time in the house of Daryatmo, a local *dukun* (curer of supernatural problems), who became the first guru in his life. Such mystical guidance always remained important to him.

He graduated from high school in 1939, working briefly in a village bank, and would later claim he lost the job because his only sarong was accidentally torn and he could not afford to replace it. The alternative version is that he was sacked for stealing clothes, and was ordered by the court to join the army as an alternative to prison.

In the Army

The only path forward for young men in what was then the Dutch East Indies—outside the tiny elite sent to college—was the army. Suharto joined the Royal Netherlands Indies army in 1940, and soon became a sergeant. When the Japanese invaded in 1942, the Dutch commander in chief, Lieutenant General Ter Poorten, surrendered precipitately. Any respect for the colonial power was lost.

Suharto, with tens of thousands of others from the disbanded force, joined Peta, the Volunteer Army of Defenders of the Motherland, whose explicit aim was to help Japan defend

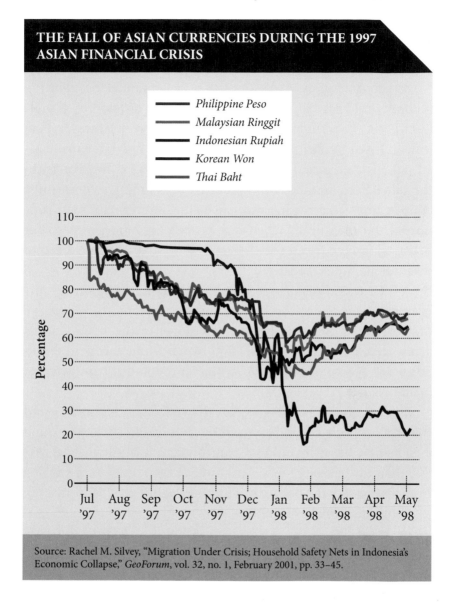

THE FALL OF ASIAN CURRENCIES DURING THE 1997 ASIAN FINANCIAL CRISIS

Philippine Peso
Malaysian Ringgit
Indonesian Rupiah
Korean Won
Thai Baht

Percentage

110
100
90
80
70
60
50
40
30
20
10
0

Jul '97 Aug '97 Sep '97 Oct '97 Nov '97 Dec '97 Jan '98 Feb '98 Mar '98 Apr '98 May '98

Source: Rachel M. Silvey, "Migration Under Crisis; Household Safety Nets in Indonesia's Economic Collapse," *GeoForum*, vol. 32, no. 1, February 2001, pp. 33–45.

Indonesia against invasion by the western allies. In fact, national-ist leaders such as Sukarno and Mohammed Hatta used support for Japan to arouse a more general sense of anti-imperialism.

The Japanese turned ex-NCOs, including Suharto, into offi-cers and gave them further military education, including lessons in the use of the samurai sword. Suharto's adulatory biographer, OG Roeder, records in *The Smiling General* (1969) that his subject was "well known for his tough, but not brutal, methods".

When, in August 1945, the Japanese surrender brought the second world war to a close, its forces were ordered by the allies to prevent an Indonesian nationalist takeover. However, Peta units refused to disarm, seizing control of several large towns.

Suharto led a raid on the Japanese garrison at Jogjakarta. In the official account, he is also credited with foiling a communist coup against Sukarno. In a more plausible interpretation, he supported the conspiracy when it appeared likely to succeed, but betrayed it once it had failed. Fact and myth are equally hard to disentangle in his career.

When Indonesia gained independence in 1949 after a four-year struggle against the Dutch, Sukarno became the country's first president. Suharto, by then a colonel in the new national army, took part in the pacification of rebellious forces in South Sulawesi, where his troops earned a reputation for extreme brutality.

Suharto and his colleagues saw themselves as operators—and the army as the mechanism—to steer Indonesian society through a transition beset by militant communism and Islam. Less visible than the senior generals around Sukarno, they were waiting in the wings for the president's uneasy coalition of Muslims, the PKI and the army to crumble.

September 30, 1965

That moment came on September 30 1965, when the PKI leader, DN Aidit (apparently acting on his own), and a small group of leftwing officers launched a botched coup in which six senior generals were killed. Suharto, who mysteriously survived, quickly suppressed the uprising.

Over the next six months, army units and local vigilante groups launched a nationwide purge of so-called communists, a catch-all label that included labour and civic leaders and thousands of others who would never have even heard of Karl Marx. Most were shot, stabbed, beaten to death or thrown down wells in acts of horrifying violence.

The purge was masterminded by Suharto, who soon persuaded President Sukarno to vest in him leadership of the armed forces, and used trusted officers to carry it out. It is thought up to 600,000 were killed.

Ascent to Power

Suharto, while professing complete loyalty to the president, quickly marginalised Sukarno. And by March 1966, Sukarno had transferred most of his power to Suharto, who became acting president a year later. By March 1968, he was formally elected president by the tame provisional parliament. Sukarno remained under house arrest till his death in 1970.

Suharto shrewdly retained Sukarno's *pancasila* ideology, first put forward as Indonesian state philosophy in 1945—the five vague principles were a belief in God, national unity, humanitarianism, social justice and democracy. He presented his own regime as a rational choice between communism and Islamism, with occasional forays against overseas Chinese business interests.

Under Suharto, Indonesia enjoyed a favourable international climate. His regime was applauded by the west for its "suppression of communism", a policy the US covertly encouraged. It also won approval from Moscow, which had regarded the PKI's close links with China with alarm.

Over the following decade, US oil companies invested more than $2bn in Indonesia's petroleum industry, accounting for 90% of the country's total production. More than 1.5 million people were "transmigrated" from Java and Bali to relieve population pressure and colonise outlying islands.

Suharto gained his biggest reward for destroying the Indonesian left when he invaded East Timor in December 1975, only a day after the US president, Gerald Ford, and his secretary of state, Henry Kissinger, had dined with him.

As secret documents obtained in 2001 by the independent Washington-based National Security Archive would reveal, Suharto asked for US "understanding if we deem it necessary to take rapid or drastic action". In reply, Ford told Suharto: "We will understand and will not press you on the issue".

New Order of Repression

Proclaiming a "new order", Suharto confined domestic politics to setpiece elections contested by two federations of former parties and an army-dominated body, Golkar, which had no party members but won 60% to 70% of the vote.

It seemed a recipe for an Iranian-style upheaval, but Suharto survived the growth of discontent through the ruthless use of an intelligence apparatus. Muslim militants were jailed and social protests suppressed. More subtly, the older politicians whom he had supplanted were allowed to form an ineffective "group of 50" in 1980.

Suharto's real talent lay in manipulating the military elite on which he relied and yet needed to divide and rule. Those he depended on most would find themselves discarded when they might threaten to become too powerful.

However, the 1990s saw a revival of labour unrest. The biggest source of dissent was a huge growth in cronyism and the blatant pursuit of financial gain by the Suharto family.

Such nepotism was not essential for the Suharto regime— it reflected his adoption of a ruling style increasingly akin to that of a traditional Javanese king. The village in which he had been born was graced with a palace, and it was ordained that he should be buried in the nearby family mausoleum, echoing the royal custom of hilltop interment.

Following nationwide protests, he resigned in May 1998, having finally lost the confidence of even his own military clique.

After a year's silence, the former president emerged to deny claims he had amassed a fortune, filing a suit against *Time* magazine for publishing detailed allegations. There were suggestions he had threatened to implicate other members of the Jakarta elite if the investigation proved too vigorous.

After suffering a stroke, his lawyers claimed he was too ill to be questioned by the attorney general. In April 2000, he was banned from leaving Jakarta. He was later ruled unfit to stand trial on physical and mental grounds.

He is survived by his six children, among them Hutomo "Tommy" Mandala Putra, who served four years in prison for hiring a hitman to assassinate the judge who had convicted him of corruption.

Indonesia Still Struggles with the Historical Memory of the 1965 Genocide

Adrian Vickers and Katharine E. McGregor

Adrian Vickers is a professor of Asian studies at the University of Wollongong. Katharine E. McGregor teaches Southeast Asian history at the University of Melbourne. In the following viewpoint, they argue that while the official history enforced by Suharto's regime has come undone, nothing has replaced it. Political tensions around the 1965 genocide remain powerful, and revisiting the events of that time provokes resistance and even violence. They conclude that it is unclear whether Indonesia will ever be able to assess its history honestly or move toward justice and reconciliation for the victims of the genocide.

During his short term as president [of Indonesia in 1999 after Suharto's fall], Abdul Wahid recognised the need to promote discussions of the PKI in the public arena as part of a process of reconciliation. Wahid, popularly known as Gus Dur, did this first by apologising for the massacres (on 13 March 2000), secondly by attempting to lift the ban on the PKI, and thirdly by mooting a South-African style Truth and Reconciliation Commission, something that had already been talked about at

Adrian Vickers and Katharine E. McGregor, "Public Debates About History: Comparative Notes from Indonesia," *History Australia*, vol. 2, no. 2, June 2005, pp. 44.1–44.13. Copyright © 2005 by Monash University Publishing. All rights reserved. Reproduced by permission.

the time of the fall of Suharto. For many Indonesian intellectuals this is the only alternative to cycles of revenge.

Struggles with Reconciliation

Long-term political rivals from the polarised years of the early 1960s, Goenawan Mohamad and Indonesia's most famous novelist, Pramoedya Ananta Toer, had very different responses to the issue of reconciliation. Pramoedya, 'an icon of the 1965 victims', rejected Gus Dur's apology, arguing that justice through legal processes was preferable to what he felt was 'mere talk by the people in power'. Goenawan's reply was to call for forgiveness and humility, because the grievances and crimes in Indonesia's past were too many to be justly resolved.

Goenawan's discussion was premised on eliciting positive individual responses to the process of reconciliation, rather than a state or national solution to the problem of how to deal with the past. Pramoedya, the only writer to present an alternative historiography during the New Order period, was well aware that history and good intentions sit badly together and was skeptical of the capacity of a new narrative to heal past wounds. Even in the South African case, which Goenawan sees as more straightforward, there are questions about a just historiography emerging from the Commission.

The reactions of the right to Gus Dur's apology show the complexity of the problem of reaching agreement on a new interpretation of the killings. As the former head of the large Islamic organization Nahdlatul Ulama (NU), an institution directly involved in the 1965 killings, Gus Dur's moves to encourage reconciliation were brave. NU's 'youth wing', Ansor, at various times headed by close relatives of Gus Dur, killed more people in East Java than Suharto's military forces. Although Gus Dur won some support from the Yogyakarta division of Ansor, his own supporters turned against him on this issue. His initiatives gave ammunition to hardline elements in Muslim politics. The majority of the parliament continued to stigmatise the left in the political parties bill of 2003, which perpetuated the 1966 ban on the PKI and tried to ban political participation by anyone deemed to be 'PKI.'

Forgetting History

In the National Assembly the rejection of any examination of 1965 was led by House Leader Akbar Tanjung, the Chair of Golkar, the political vehicle of the New Order [Suharto's political program]. Tanjung was later convicted of corruption. His allies included a large section of Nahdlatul Ulama and various military and ex-military leaders. Rather than confront the issues of the killings, Tanjung and his allies either argued that history should be ignored ('we should look to the future' said Tanjung), or they resorted to older readings of history. When the killings were discussed, Muslim groups attributed responsibility to the communists. They argued that in 1948, during a crucial incident in the Indonesian Revolution known as the 'Madiun Affair', Muslims had been victims of communist aggression. The only detailed account of 1948 communist atrocities against Muslims, produced during the New Order period, documented how over 200 Muslims were killed by communists, without mentioning that Muslim militias and right-wing military killed at least 20,000 communists in the aftermath of the Madiun Affair. On the basis of such accounts, assertions of the brutality of communists were taken for granted.

During Gus Dur's attempts at reconciliation, 'anticommunist groups', apparently a combination of quasi-military groups and hired thugs of the kind employed by the New Order, carried out raids on bookstores and book burnings. Commenting on these, a sociologist who did not approve of the book burnings nevertheless repeated the Islamic line, 'What the PKI did in the past to our people [in 1948, but also with the killings of the Generals in 1965] was too traumatic for the families of the victims'. Here we see evidence of the persistence of New Order narratives where they continue to serve the interests of different groups.

In line with the New Order version of history, the commemoration of suppression of the PKI, called 'The Day of the Sacred Power of the Five Principles' (*Hari Kesaktian Pancasila*) by the New Order, was salvaged as 'Commemoration Day for the Betrayal of the Five Principles' ('*Peringatan Hari Pengkhianatan [terhadap] Pancasila*'). Although this move was meant to undermine New Order interpretations of the day as sacralising the Five Principles, it was all too easily appropriated by the Islamic right. Islamic groups had always disapproved of the idea of Pancasila being 'sacred' (the standard, but not necessarily correct, translation of *sakti* which means something like 'mystical power or energy'), so they already saw the move as an answer to their lobbying. Further . . . the New Order had already prepared the way for such an appropriation by cultivating a deliberately Islamic flavour to the celebrations in the 1990s. The day has been left ambiguous, with no clear agency of 'betrayal' identified. The majority of people brought up on New Order propaganda films such as the *Treachery of the 30th September Movement* would still see the PKI as the betrayers, although the Muslim groups involved in protests around the naming also implied that the New Order had betrayed the memory of the PKI's killings of Muslims in 1948.

Fear of Victims

Indonesian academics have been reluctant to give the PKI the status of 'victims'. Two Indonesian academics who had written doctoral dissertations on the killings, Iwan Sujatmiko and Hermawan Sulistyo, presented the PKI unsympathetically in discussions of their research for Indonesian audiences. Sulistyo, who was close to Gus Dur, tended towards accepting the view of his NU sources, while Sujatmiko explicitly argued that the destruction of the PKI was a logical consequence of their own revolutionary strategy . . . the fall of the New Order will not automatically permit [*membenarkan* (!)] former members of the PKI and their sympathisers to whitewash [*pamutihan*] the history of the PKI's destruction. Their efforts to depict the *PKI* as a bunker

Indonesian students burn a photo of former president Suharto during a 2005 demonstration in Jakarta marking the seventh anniversary of the dictator's fall. © Adek Berry/AFP/Getty Images.

[*kubu*] on the side of 'peace' and 'without fault' is at odds with the realities of the history of that time [*sejarah saat itu*]. Partly motivated by fear of the book burnings and threats to members of the media made especially by violent groups who claimed to act in the name of Islam, the majority of the media fell into line with this view.

Public intellectuals were right to problematise the status of the PKI, as Goenawan Mohamad so clearly explained in his response to Pramoedya:

> In an age when the victim is easily sanctified, one who thinks himself of a higher degree of victimisation will, with ease, also believe in the right to become the ultimate arbiter of justice. But, as with every claim to sanctity, this too could give rise to arbitrariness. Mandela knew this . . . [He has] humbled [himself].

But a problem remains. Denying victimhood to those labelled PKI licenses some Islamic groups to claim the exclusive status of victims. As well as being the victims of Madiun, these groups also claim to be victims of the New Order, especially in 1984 when up to 500 Muslims were killed by the military in riots in North Jakarta known as the Tanjung Priok Affair. The status of Indonesian Islam as a 'majority with a minority mentality', to quote W.F. Wertheim's summative phrase, makes the manipulation of Islamic victimhood one of the easiest tools for politicians to use. So in 1996 modernist Muslim intellectual Adi Sasono could attack Gus Dur for being too close to Benny Murdani, the (Christian) military leader whom Muslims hold responsible for Tanjung Priok. Likewise in 1988 Suharto's son-in-law was able to harness Muslim hardliners to manipulate theories of conspiracies by 'the CIA (Amerika), Mossad (Jews), the Vatican and overseas Chinese' to incite murder and rape of ethnic Chinese Indonesians. Islamic groups have been simultaneously urged to support their Islamic brethren in Maluku and Palestine, and to defend, '*membela*', Islam against the threat to it from the West.

Islam in Indonesia is not, however, monolithic, despite claims by some leaders to speak on behalf of all Muslims. Different Muslims groups hold radically different positions in the historiographic debates. Those who were of the left have continued to produce accounts of the killings, of their imprisonment by the New Order, and of their continued suppression in post-New Order Indonesia. From the side of Gus Dur's followers in the NU has come an important attempt to keep the reconciliation process going. The NU journal *Afkar*, for example, published a special issue on the Coup and the killings that attempted to provide a more nuanced version of what happened on 30th September, to discuss the motivations of those members of NU who took part in the killings, and to explore the theological basis of the reconciliation process. A number of historians see as the best approach to the problem of reconciliation a view of both Muslims and leftists as victims of common New Order oppression, the position adopted by the organisation Syarikat which was founded in 2000 specifically for the purpose of reconciling members of Ansor and the families of victims of the killings.

The Problem of 'National History' and Historiography

The dominant view of history underlying these discussions is that it is a raw tool of politics. Over the last few years opposition to the standard New Order version of history has been about the only thing that historians can agree on. This opposition included demonstrations in which the authorised *National History* (*Sejarah Nasional Indonesia*) was burned.

Megawati's Vice President, Hamzah Haz, always ready to play the Islamic card, called for the banning of the book *I Am Proud to be the Child of a Communist* (Proletariyati 2002) on the grounds that 'the title of this book is in opposition to state ideology which refuses the teachings of communism'. Unwittingly, and with unintended irony, Haz identified the chief problem. With the removal of the authority of the New Order account of history, there is no longer a clear account of what constitutes 'state ideology', and what historical base that ideology rests upon.

Attempts to produce an officially-authorised history have as yet come to nothing. Juwono Sudarsono, who served in the last Suharto cabinet and then became Habibie's education minister, made the positive step of opening up the national education history curriculum during 1998. He organised consultative seminars during October of that year, aimed at allowing a variety of historians to contribute to overturning the New Order's curriculum, which as Juwono observed, gave priority to the military's role as principal actor in history. School teachers had asked for the correct answers so they could teach history, although they did not reflect on what the questions might be.

Juwono and others complained about a history curriculum that was Suharto-centred. The discussions began with Juwono promoting the idea of an 'objective' history. Or to be more precise, he used the key words 'objective, factual, more balanced, and in proportion' (*objektif, wajar, lebih berimbang, dan lebih proporsional*). These terms are common rhetorical markers in Indonesian polemics, having the main function of discrediting one's opponents. Juwono further identified the problem of concentration on 'historical figures' (*tokoh*) as a major barrier not only to history but also to the establishment of the supremacy of the law and the constitution.

Media reports of the subsequent discussions included commentaries by the dominant school of history, that of Gadjah Mada University, represented by some of the nation's foremost social historians, but the Indonesian Historians' Society (*Masyarakat Sejarahwan Indonesia*) quickly became the main body quoted, with their Head, Taufik Abdullah, being the person most often mentioned after novelist Pramoedya Ananta Toer. Azyumardi Azra, Professor at the Islamic University Syarief Hidayatullah, Jakarta, attempted to bridge the gap between popular and professional history by suggesting that history is not the preserve of professional historians—'informal historians' also have a role to play. History should not, he says, be taught as something that happened long ago ['*di masa silam*'], but rather be a 'living history' [English used] which is a form of 'contemporary history'. Living history is useful [*bermanfaat*] to broaden and enrich collective memory ['*ingatan kolektif*'].

Memory and Revenge

Memory was a major historiographical concern within the debates. Goenawan Mohamad had already spoken of the issues around 1965 as being problems of 'the persistence of memory'. Azra's appeal to collective memory was repeated by most of the historians contributing to the debate. Taufik Abdullah worried, however, that collective memory would feed feelings of the need for revenge. Taufik repeated the dominant Indonesian historiographic focus on 'events' (*peristiwa*) while avoiding the complementary interest in great men. He argued that it is normal for society to remember and forget, but that the New Order used the recollection of events loaded with revenge to legitimate their power. His solution was to turn away from strategies of collective memory obsessed with legitimating power. Instead the government should order (*menata*) the collective memory of society through concentration on positive events. His example was that regions should promote their own histories of the coming of Islam 'as an event full of wonder rather than conflict'.

'Order' was an unusual term to use in this discussion. Most of the media commentaries on history consistently referred to the idea of 'straightening (*meluruskan*) history'. For example the major daily *Kompas* reports of the 2000 Papuan People's Congress, to discuss West Papuan independence, cited the late Theys Eluay's opening speech as being about how 'Papua's history had been twisted' ('*Sejarah Papua Dibelokkan*'). The congress's leaders were said to wish to 'straighten' (*luruskan*) the history of Papua. Syamdani's earlier mentioned book had a similar aim. He specifically elevated narratives that he felt were true ('*benar*'), as against Suharto's lies, '*bohong*.'

Syamdani is a journalist, so it would be unfair to expect him to meet standards of academic historiography. The same cannot be said for Asvi Warman Adam, a leading historian from the premier national research body the Indonesian Institute of the Sciences, LIPI. Adam constantly intervenes in media debates on history using his authority as a qualified historian. In 2004 Adam published a history of the Suharto period which claimed to achieve a just account of that era. His monograph attempted both to give a definitive account of the New Order and to intervene directly in the current political situation, at a time when moves to prosecute Suharto for his crimes had stalled. Adam provided a series of mini-essays connecting the violence of the New Order with the current political situation in Indonesia. Sadly his book was poorly referenced; most of the few footnotes have titles followed by 'source that cannot be traced'. Although Adam's attempt to dismantle Suharto's self-made image may well please Indonesian readers in the current anti-Suharto climate, his work is marred by a lack of commitment to an even-handed treatment of the evidence. This position underpins Adam's *ad hominem* critique of Australian historian R.E. Elson's biography of Suharto, on the basis that anything that does not tear down Suharto must be defending him. The ploy of attacking a writer's background rather than addressing his or her work is a common one in these debates, a problem that is not unique to Indonesian public history.

Truth, Accuracy, and Cynicism

Three decades of the New Order have left Indonesians cynical about truth and accuracy. Commentators argue that 'only Americans care about methodology anyway' and that it is permissible for newspapers to publish fabrications and rumours without qualification—no Jews were killed in New York on September 11, the US bombed Kuta. Scholars working outside Indonesia have access to extensive library and archival collections on Indonesia, but inside the nation poor record-keeping, inadequate funding and a culture of closely guarded sensitive archives has made it very difficult for Indonesian historians to reconstruct the past independently.

An activist who worked outside the universities, Hilmar Farid (2002), has researched social history and written in a variety of media on historiography. In a paper on historiography published on-line, he pointed out that the term '*meluruskan*' means that history has been written 'crookedly', i.e. manipulated (*dimanipulasi*). While he agreed that there was already clear evidence that this was done by the New Order, he warned that historians understand that all historical writing is marked by omissions and weaknesses (*kekurangan dan kelemahan*) which result from processes of interpretation rather than deliberate falsification. To have a 'straight' (*lurus*) history you have to have an authority that establishes and fixes its straightness ['*adanya orotitas (kekuasaan) yang bisa menetapkan dan memastikan . . .*'] As Farid observed, however, the official New Order accounts were based on 'outright factual errors' (*fakta-fakta yang keliru sama sekali*) and the concealing of facts which did not support their assertions (*dan juga penggelapan fakta-fakta yang tidak mendukung kesimpulannya*). So as well as countering factual errors, he notes, there is a need to look at what remains unsaid. Farid went on to argue that the procedures for countering New Order arguments are problematic, because they began from the *a priori* assumptions established by the New Order. His example was that when opponents of the New Order wish to counter the official account that the Coup was 'manipulated by the Communist Party' (*didalangi oleh PKI*), they look for evidence to prove their argument that the PKI was not the 'puppeteer' and ignore evidence to the contrary. In this Farid's argument lined up with Goenawan's, that we should also critically examine PKI claims to victimhood. While arguing for alternative directions in history writing, based on careful documentation and use of sources, he said those directions should be towards opening up new perspectives and questions. His warning about creating a new orthodoxy was important for its recognition that Indonesian historical discourse is not far removed from the authoritarian tendencies of the New Order. Here, and in his other activities, Farid argued that the whole of Indonesian historiography should restart, from the bottom up. In much the same vein the director of history at the Ministry of National Education called in 2001 for the public to be the ones who re-wrote the National History so that it would become more of a dialogue in society.

A New Start

Farid's vision of a total reconstruction of Indonesian historiography is the clearest presentation of a view that others hint at. Only the few Indonesian feminist historians have matched this call in their argument that all aspects of Indonesian history need to be reconsidered if the roles of women are to receive proper recognition. Most of these feminist historians operate outside the academic mainstream, especially through Forum Kerja Budaya (in which Farid is active), but their calls were joined in 2002 by the Minister for Women's Empowerment, Sri Redjeki Sumaryoto.

Indonesian history writing is poised at a critical juncture. As yet the committees convened by successive governments have not produced a new national history, although the promise is there. As [Gerry] Van Klinken observes historians from an earlier generation such as Soedjatmoko rejected the use of history to promote nationalism. In the media commentaries on history, and particularly on the national history curriculum, there is an unspoken tension. On the one hand there is a recognition that without an agreed national history there can be no rejuvenation of nationalism, but on the other there is the desire for a general, pluralist, people's history. The end of singular narratives about the past may well represent a move towards the democratisation of history in Indonesia. The pluralist view is unintentionally served by the on-going political conflicts manifested in history writing, because as yet no single authority has been able to claim 'ownership' of history.

In this new climate in which history is up for grabs, there are no standards, however, for verifying evidence. 'History proves' anything one wants. Historians are fighting to maintain the integrity, if not the credibility, of their profession.

CHAPTER 3

Personal Narratives

Chapter Exercises

1. **Writing Prompt**

   Imagine your parents were imprisoned as Communists in Indonesia in 1965. Write a one-page diary entry discussing the prejudice and difficulties you face.

2. **Group Activity**

   Form groups and develop five oral history questions you would ask of individuals who participated in the 1965 killings in Indonesia.

1

An Indonesian Catholic Recalls His Experiences as an Anti-Communist Before 1965

Jusuf Wanandi

Jusuf Wanandi co-founded the Centre for Strategic and International Studies and served as president director of the Jakarta Post *and chairman of Praesetiya Mulya Business School. In the following viewpoint, he discusses his time working with Catholic groups prior to the September 30, 1965, coup. He discusses the power maneuvers of the Indonesian Communist Party (PKI), and the fear and uncertainty about the outcome of the coup for himself, his family, and the Catholic community, which was opposed to the Communists.*

By then we knew that a crisis was in the offing. Not only was Sukarno sick, but we knew that the PKI was making plans. From our informant, we had heard the doctors had told [Communist Party leader Dipa Nusantara] Aidit: "Sukarno is sick. He cannot hold on very long. Whatever you have to do, do it now." That was in the middle of August, and by the end of the month, the PKI had begun to prepare its next move.

Jusuf Wanandi, *Shades of Grey: A Political Memoir of Modern Indonesia 1965–1998.* Equinox Publishing, 2012, pp. 43–47. Copyright © 2012 by Equinox Publishing. All rights reserved. Reproduced by permission.

The PKI Moves

PKI's problem remained the superior power of the Army. So its solution, reached sometime in the second half of August by the PKI Politburo, was in some ways an ingenious one: Create the appearance of a putsch by young and progressive officers within the Army. A Special Bureau would be formed, distanced from the PKI's Politburo and Central Committee, neither of which would be formally involved. The purported goal would be to rid Indonesia of CIA spies and corrupt capitalist bureaucrats from the Army command. Supporting them would be mass movements to push for these *kabir* ("capitalist bureaucrats") to be brought before people's tribunals to be accused, judged and sentenced. Aidit would head the bureau; Sjam Kamaruzaman its chief operator. Those PKI members who had infiltrated the Army would be the ones to carry out the putsch under the leadership of Lt. Col. Untung of the Tjakrabirawa, the Presidential Guards Brigade. The PKI could say, as it would later: We were not involved. And it would be, at least partly, true.

Most of this we heard through our informant, but key details were confused or missing, which would later hamper our attempts to warn the leadership of what was about to happen. We didn't know the Aidit/Sjam unit was called the Special Bureau, and we didn't know the identity of the Army officers involved, or the units. We didn't know who their targets in the Army would be. We thought they would be the most corrupt officers, such as those in state enterprises taken over by the PKI in late 1957, nationalised in 1958 and then taken over again by the Army. We thought there might be mass demonstrations and these figures would be brought in front of the masses to be judged and sentenced as had happened in 1950–53 in China after the CCP [Chinese Communist Party] won in 1949. Capitalist bureaucrats in front of the People's Court: "*Ini bangsat, ini mencuri, ini CIA, bagaimana? Kita adili dial Hancurkan!*" (This is a crook, this is a thief, this is CIA. What are we going to do? Let's put them on trial! Destroy!) And then you have 100,000 people scouring the streets. This is what we had expected, and why we were preparing to go into hiding ourselves. We, too, would be taken by surprise.

It was not hard for us to piece together a general picture that something was afoot. In mid-September we heard that the PKI Secretariat had been told to look for safe houses for its leaders and put the PKI documents in secure places. Other documents were destroyed. PKI figures were starting to go underground. All the statements of PKI leaders, such as one from Central Committee member Anwar Sanusi, who wrote in the 30 September edition of the *Bintang Timur* daily that the country was in a "state of advanced pregnancy, and soon something important is going to be delivered" showed that they expected something dramatic to happen. . . .

Catholics Organize

After getting all this intelligence about what the PKI was planning—clearly something serious was afoot, but how and when was unclear—Harry Tjan went to see General Abdul Haris Nasution, then the Chief of Staff of the Armed Forces and Coordinating Minister for Security and Defence. He was accompanied by Ignatius Joseph Kasimo Hendrowahyono, chairman of the advisory board of the Catholic Party whose blessing we needed to gain support from the party.

Seeing the PKI mobilising, we Catholics had done what we could. Since 1964 we had been training two groups of cadres of student leaders and academics in Gunung Sahari and we had in recent weeks tried to consolidate them as quickly as we could. Our Muslim allies at HMI [the Muslim students' association] had done the same thing at Mega Mendung, outside Bogor, at the residence of NU [a Sunni Islam group] Vice Chairman Subchan Zaenuri Erfan. We were the only two non-communist groups doing so.

Kasimo and Harry Tjan told Nasution what we knew about the plan of the PKI, and asked what should be done—especially after knowing that the Communist Youth and Gerwani [Indonesian Women's Movement] were being trained by the Air Force at Halim.

"Why have all these trainings been going on for so many months and we were not trained?" Harry Tjan asked. "How can you let that happen?"

Nasution's answer was disappointing—and, in the scheme of things, devastating for him personally. Since Omar Dhani, the Commander of the Air Force, was also a member of Bung Karno's Cabinet ["Bung Karno" is another name for Sukarno] and therefore of the same rank as himself, there was nothing he could do, he said.

"What can I do?" Nasution said. "I am only a minister and the one who is training them is also another minister."

"If that's the case," Harry Tjan said, "then you train us too! HMI and we have been training ourselves, but because our knowledge is limited, if it comes down to a physical confrontation, we will be outmatched."

"OK," Nasution said. "You come back on Monday. Let me see what I can do." Following that meeting, I joined Harry Tjan when, at around midday, he went to see Subchan, who was also the HMI leader, at his office on Jalan Cikini Raya. Mar'ie Muhammad, vice president of HMI, was there. We told them about the meeting with Nasution and discussed how to prepare our students to be trained in accordance with Nasution's promise. We weren't to know that the putsch was only a few hours away.

We were not the only ones suspecting something was afoot. General Yani was warned by his intelligence officer Suparman of a possible action by the PKI. He sent a special team to protect Yani at his residence in Menteng, but Yani sent the guards back. "If the PKI dare to do anything," Yani roared, "I will wipe them out." He was one of the first to be killed.

The Coup Comes

I did not hear the proclamation broadcast on state radio at 7 A.M. on 1 October 1965 because I was washing my car—a new Toyota jeep I had borrowed from the State Secretariat under Presidential Secretary Djamin. I left my home on Jalan Kartini and drove to

Jusuf Wanandi (seen in a 2002 photograph) was among those in the Catholic community opposed to the Communists and the Indonesian coup. © Rick Maiman/AFP/Getty Images.

work as normal at around 10 A.M. The roads were as busy as ever: nothing was visibly untoward at that point. On the way, I had planned to stop at the Documentation Centre at Jalan Gunung Sahari, when Harry Tjan, riding on the back of a motorbike, flagged me down a few houses away from the centre. He told me about the radio broadcast, about how Lt. Col. Untung had talked of a Generals' Council that had planned a coup. The government had been abolished, the broadcast had said, and Untung was in charge. A Revolutionary Council would soon be announced. The bulletin also reported the capture of some "contra-revolutionary generals, capitalist-bureaucrats and spies of the CIA." Sukarno was not mentioned at all in the announcement. Harry Tjan also told me something else.

"They're saying there's been shooting at Nasution's and Yani's homes," he said. Since I had a license to enter the Palace, he asked me to find out whether Sukarno was there. It was about 11 A.M.

On the way, I saw dozens of soldiers positioned around the Palace with white ribbon on their left shoulder, about 20cm long and 2-to-3cm wide. They were just standing around, not doing anything. I drove my jeep to the special pump where I was allowed to get petrol—I wasn't sure when I was going to be able to do so again—and then went to the building next door to the Palace, occupied by the State Secretary, where I met Pak Djamin, the President's secretary. I chatted around the subject for as long as I could before asking him where the President was.

"*Pak, kenapa tidak ada orang? Ke mana Pak Presiden? Ke mana Bung Karno?*" (Why is there nobody here? Where's the president? Where's Bung Karno?) Djamin, a fine and loyal man, replied: "I also don't know. But definitely he's in a safe place. But if you ask me where, I don't know."

I knew he was pretending, but I could understand his need for secrecy. And I too had to pretend to Pak Djamin that I was there in sympathy with him and to support Bung Karno. But I could tell that he did not want to talk. I sat around for an hour and a half, and tried to talk about anything else under the sun before gently asking again. Each time, Djamin would say, "I don't know."

Bung Karno was not in the Palace, that was for sure, because it looked empty except for soldiers surrounding it. I stayed with Pak Djamin for two hours and left at 1:30 P.M. for Jalan Sam Ratulangi, PMKRI's headquarters near what was then the Immigration Office. By now the streets were very empty. It was eerie.

Uncertainty and Fear Take Over

There I found Harry Tjan, who had lived there earlier during his student days. Although I had only been away a couple of hours, Harry and my friends at the Catholic Student Union Centre (Margasiswa) were very worried about what could happen to me, in a Palace surrounded supposedly by the "Revolutionary Council" troops under Lt. Col. Untung. As we discussed what I had seen and heard, a second announcement came over the radio at 2 P.M.

Untung named his Revolutionary Council, which was supposedly installed as the New Temporary Government of Indonesia. It consisted of 45 people from all walks of life. There were no Catholics among them. Sukarno was again not mentioned. Sukarno would always name one or two Catholics in any list of appointments to an important institution, so it was clear to us who was behind this. "It has to be the PKI." Coupled with our knowledge from our informant, we had expected that they would make a move. But it was still far from clear how the mass-actions of dealing justice to this "contra-revolutionary clique of corrupt capitalist-bureaucrats" would take place.

We needed to act quickly. Our priority was to ensure Pak Kasimo's safety. If they eliminated him, there would be no leadership in the Catholic community. So we took him to a friend's house on Jalan Kwitang, Central Jakarta, a safe house we had set up earlier. . . . We also tried to contact as many of our cadres as possible and directed them to our headquarters.

Harry and I decided we would stay on at Margasiswa. We did not know then that we would stay there for more than six months. I was 27 years old, married and blessed with two children: Yudi and Ari. Unable to take care of them myself, I took them to my father-in-law's house and asked him to take care of my family for now. Harry had to postpone his wedding to Trees; in the end he could only have a small reception at Margasiswa in October instead of September. He had to stay at Margasiswa even during his honeymoon. We really had no idea when this would finish, and of course no idea whether we would win or not.

A Western Observer Describes the Violence of 1965

John Hughes

John Hughes was the first American correspondent into Jakarta after the September 30, 1965, coup. In the following viewpoint, he describes the anti-Communist violence in Java, basing his account on personal interviews and observations. Hughes is the author of The End of Sukarno: A Coup That Misfired: A Purge That Ran Wild.

On a hill overlooking Java's volcano-studded central plain stands the famous temple of Borobudur.

It is a monument of grandeur, its gray stone turned mellow green in many parts by centuries of tropical climate. From a base whose sides are more than a hundred yards long, it climbs regally upwards in a series of curved terraces to a central dome. This is surrounded by more than five hundred carved stone Buddhas, some of them set in niches, others protected by massive bell-like structures of latticed stone. Its terraces are faced with stone relief panels carved in exquisite detail.

Borobudur is not, perhaps, as splendid as Angkor, the ruins of the ancient capital of the Khmer empire in Cambodia, but dating from the late 8th or early 9th century, it is one of Asia's great relics and testimony enough to the great cultural history of the Javanese people.

Around Borobudur the countryside seems tranquil enough. As the young rice shoots up in the flooded paddies, there is vivid green as far as the eye can see. The land is overcrowded, but this garden of Java is clearly lush and fertile. In the little towns, pony carts clatter along with a tinkling of bells. Heavier loads, of rice and sugar cane and coconuts and swaying bamboo poles, are dragged by massive, serene, humped white cattle. And at the end of a day's plowing, the gray water buffaloes sink into some pool in an ecstasy of sucking, squelching, splashing muddiness.

There is a saying in Java that happiness is a home, a wife, and a singing bird. And so, outside the simple little houses of plaited bamboo strips, there is often a pole, atop which hangs a birdcage with a brilliantly colored bird in it trilling merrily away. With all the formality of a national flag being raised and lowered outside some building of state, the bird is hoisted by pulley to the top of its pole at dawn, then hauled down again at dusk when people start lighting up their flickering little coconut-oil lamps.

Then, too, come marching home in a flurry of clucking self-importance the fat white ducks, which have spent the day pecking away in the fields. They are not as clever as they think, for they are really the prisoners of an urchin who carries a stick with a piece of tattered white cloth tied to it. Like soldiers trained only to obey, they follow that little piece of white cloth all day. When their youthful keeper rams his stick into the muddy earth and leaves the cloth flying, they never stray beyond sight of it.

Mass Violence Ends the Happiness

Yet for all the ancient estheticism of Borobudur, and the apparent tranquility of the surrounding countryside, this island of Java in the last months of 1965 was the scene of one of history's worst orgies of slashing, shooting, chopping violence. Thousands of Indonesians who were members of the Communist Party, or who supported it, or who were suspected of supporting it, or who were said by somebody to have supported it, were put ruthlessly to death. In the mayhem, people innocent of Communist affiliations were killed too, sometimes by mistake, sometimes because their old enemies were paying off grudges in the guise of an anti-Communist campaign.

Not many miles from Borobudur there took place a bloody massacre under the very walls of another religious shrine, the 9th-century temple of Loro Djonggrang (Slender Virgin) at Prambanan. Moslem youths were attacked there by Communist members of the Pemuda Rakjat [the youth wing of the PKI]: A number of Moslems were killed and quickly buried. When their friends and families came looking for the bodies to transfer them to another burial place with proper religious rites, the Pemuda Rakjat resisted. The Moslems called in the army to help, and the military say they killed fifty Communists in the battle that ensued, but a knowledgeable resident of the area says the retaliation did not stop there. For weeks afterwards, he says, the army ferreted out Communist supporters and seized them. Each night under the temple's moonlit walls about three hundred people were killed by the army's guns and buried in unmarked mass graves.

In Central Java the army seems to have exercised broad control over the blood bath, although many civilians were also recruited to kill Communists. In East Java, the mass execution of Communists was largely handed over to civilians, mainly the black-shirted Ansor youth of the Nahdatul Ulama (Moslem Teachers' Party), who killed with fanatical relish.

Thus in Central Java the prisons quickly filled up as the army went through the motions of arresting and screening Communist suspects. Schools and military compounds were turned into makeshift jails. Political prisoners were even jammed into the Jogjakarta building that had been used to house the Thomas Jefferson Library of the USIS [United States Information Service] until the Indonesian government closed it down at the height of the anti-American campaign.

They Killed Like Pigs

No trials followed the mass arrests. Punishment was arbitrary and without appeal. Prisoners' names would be checked off against a seized Communist Party membership list, or against information supplied by informers. Those guilty of Communist affiliation were marked for execution. Usually at night, the army trucks would rumble up, and the doomed men would be marched into them at gunpoint. Then they would be driven a few miles out of town to some discreet spot chosen as the place of execution. Sometimes local villagers had already been ordered to dig big pits for the bodies. At other times, the prisoners themselves would be set to digging their graves.

Then they would be killed. If the army was in charge, death usually came with a volley of gunfire. But often the army would hand over batches of prisoners to anti-Communist groups. Then execution would be usually by knife or the broad-bladed sickles used by many Javanese for work in the fields. Many Communists were decapitated as they knelt, thumbs tied behind their backs, on the brink of their graves.

One young Indonesian I know, invited to join the killer gangs, was asked, "How will you kill, with knife or gun? Just choose your weapon, and we'll give you what you need."

The execution of Communists, however, did not always follow this pattern of crude selection from suspect lists, even when the army was in control. As the troops swept through Central Java in their "weeding out" campaign, they would be led to villages and individuals by anti-Communist informers. In cases where informers pinpointed a village as being 100 percent Communist, everyone in it died, except the youngest children. Says one nauseated Indonesian professor at Jogjakarta's Gadjah Mada University, "The anti-Communists certainly had a grudge. But there was no need to kill children, too. In one family, women, children over six, everybody was killed. And they call themselves religious people. But they killed like pigs."

Within villages, anti-Communists were assigned to eliminate Communists. It was easy for them to pick out their targets, for in such tight little communities the political views of each man were well known. Sometimes anti-Communist villages were assigned to eliminate Communist villages. In these instances, brother might often be set against brother. Many handed the names of Communist members of their family to the army so that the soldiers, rather than they, would carry out the executions.

For the historian who may one day seek to record the events of these times, there is an accumulation of grisly lore. There is the story, for example, told by soldiers riding through one Central Javanese village in their open jeep. Laughing children who had been kicking a round bundle around in the dirt shouted and waved and tossed the package into the back of the jeep. When the soldiers opened it, they found its contents to be a human head.

Certainly there were instances where heads were impaled on stakes and publicly displayed as a deterrent to further Communist activity.

No One Will Speak

Yet now as the blood bath fades into history, there seems increasing reluctance on the part of many Indonesians to admit that they themselves took part in any killings. A year after the coup, I talked in the former Communist stronghold of Solo with a group of Moslem students who had been active in the anti-Communist campaign. In detail they told me how the Communists had initially held the town, of how the grip had been broken, and of how Communists were hounded down in later months. For my concluding question I asked them directly whether any of them had taken part in the executions. As I expected, there was an embarrassed silence, then a lengthy exchange in Indonesian between one of the young men and my interpreter. "No," said my interpreter, "they say they were not involved in the killings themselves."

Later my interpreter gave me the real gist of the exchange. The student who had done the talking had not wanted the visiting correspondent to know of his own part in the executions. But actually, he told my interpreter, he had drawn weapons with other students from the para-commandos. Under their instructions he himself had killed more than a dozen Communists.

Student was set against student, professor against professor, as well as villager against villager. Among the ranks of Gadjah Mada University's 24,000 students there were many gaps when the student body reassembled after the October coup and subsequent wave of killings. Nobody needed to ask what had happened to the missing young men, nor to the professors who so quietly disappeared during the anti-Communist purge.

Throughout Central Java the story was the same, of missing mayors and municipal councilors and headmen from villages and towns known for their Communist allegiance.

Some may have been dumped into the underground river at Wonosari, not far from Jogjakarta, which was used to dispose of many bodies, according to Moslem student leaders. Said one of them to me, "It's a big river, and fast-flowing. There was no problem about it clogging up. The bodies were just whisked away with the current underground. I suppose some were eaten by fishes. The rest would have been swept out to sea."

While all this went on, the handful of foreigners in the region looked on aghast. The Japanese manager of the new, government owned hotel in Jogjakarta was told by military authorities one day to stay in, behind closed doors, as there would be shooting in the area behind the hotel. There was, and thirteen of his employees were killed.

A little later the authorities made another request. Could the military borrow his big food truck, with its hotel driver, for a few days? The manager agreed, but within 48 hours the driver was back, shaken and determined to drive no more for the military. The truck, he revealed, was being used to transport dead bodies. The manager protested, and got his truck back. A little later he took delivery of some special refrigerator trucks, to be used to ship in frozen food from the port of Surabaya. Again the army asked whether the trucks could be borrowed. This time they got an emphatic refusal.

So many people were being killed that disposal of the bodies was a serious problem. In the little coastal town of Tjirebon, according to residents, the anti-Communists set up a guillotine that worked steadily throughout the day, day after day.

But the most savage slaughter in Java was in the island's eastern region where Moslem fanatics were turned loose on the Communists apparently with little military supervision.

Ansor Members Deal Final Punishment

In East Java there was no overcrowding problem in the prisons. Without the army to go through the formality of arrest, the Ansor [a Muslim youth organization] youth dealt out instant and final punishment to their Communist enemies. Says one army general stationed in the area at the time, "There are about three thousand villages in East Java. Each of them had Communist Party members. I'd say each of them lost about ten to fifteen people as the Ansor people swept through. That means between thirty and forty-five thousand people were killed in East Java. But it could have been as high as a hundred thousand."

In the beginning, known Communist officials were quickly put to death. Then began a systematic sweep through [of] the villages. At night the killer patrols would check from house to house. Everybody was invited to identify himself and declare his politics. If he was not a member of any party, he had to prove it, and quickly. If he was a member of a nationalist or Moslem or some other non-Communist Party, he had to produce his membership card. If he turned out to be a member of the Communist Party, he was marched away to certain death, probably that very night.

In East Java the Moslem youth did not have the authority, as did the army in Central Java, to order villagers to dig mass graves, so those to be executed were often marched into the fields and there made to dig their own graves before falling to the knife and the sickle. Sometimes the execution site was the bed of a sandy river, where shallow pits could quickly be scooped out. There seems little doubt that in their haste the executioners sometimes buried some people who were still living.

But often there was neither time, opportunity, nor inclination to bury the dead. Then they were tossed into rivers. So many bodies came floating down the Brantas River that villagers downstream stopped eating fish from the river for fear some might contain a human finger or other portion of a decomposing body. One village lodged a formal protest with the authorities, claiming that the logjam of bodies posed a health hazard.

In the port city of Surabaya townsfolk were ordered to clear the bodies that washed up on the riverbanks. The British consul one morning found several bodies on the riverbank next to his garden. Still today, citizens point out a bridge, or a curve in the river, where they say the corpses were piled up in dozens.

Matter-of-factly, and unemotionally, one of the Ansor leaders long after the bloody events explained to me his organization's viewpoint. "We were taking revenge," he said, "not only for the Communists' involvement in the coup, but for their activities against us over the years.

"At Madiun, in 1948, the Communists rebelled and were smashed. But they set about organizing again. By 1963 they were very strong and very active again, in Central and East Java. In the east they attacked Ansor, and it was a pretty one-sided action. The army had only three battalions of troops in East Java, two of infantry and one of cavalry [armor]. So we Ansor people had no protection. There was physical fighting. The Communist Party took our land. Tension was rising. This [the 1965 coup and the succeeding purge] was simply the climax."

Greeting Death Like Frightened Birds

According to this Ansor spokesman, when members of his organization first moved against the Communist Party in East

Java, they discovered documents implicating the Communists in the abortive coup. "So from October to January," he continued, "we took our revenge. We knew who were Communists, and we would go to the villages and *kampongs* and kill them. The people just went wild against the Communists."

He had no hesitation about admitting his own part in some of the executions. "*At Djombang*, on November first, I was leader of an Ansor group," he explained. "The army handed over to us twenty Communists they had arrested. We knew what to do. We took them to another place where we killed them. They were not difficult to kill. They died like frightened birds.

"We'd already dug a hole for them. We killed them with knives. Guns would have been too noisy there. They would have panicked the local people. We keep quiet about where the graves are, otherwise the families might try to find them. In that particular case we dug the graves deep, so they could not be discovered."

Much of the time, he suggested, the Communists went quietly to their deaths. Sometimes, as he told it, they even cooperated. "There was an instance," he related, "where a Communist was kneeling to have his head cut off. The executioner told him, 'Lift up your head a little, so I can cut better.' The man about to die immediately lifted his head to help his executioner."

Did the Communists sometimes resist? "They did," he said, "fight back here and there, but much of the time they just seemed to crumple up and give in. There was one time, for example, where four Ansor youth came on fifteen Pemuda Rakjat boys who were armed. The Communists could have given our boys a bad time, but our boys called on them to surrender, to give up their arms. They did, and we got them."

Not all those involved in the orgy of killing could take it so quietly afterwards as this Ansor leader, however. One Indonesian acquaintance of mine has a friend who went insane because he had killed so many times. Another has violent nightmares each time he tries to sleep. A doctor in East Java tells of patients who see the faces of their victims in their sleep.

One place where the Communists did strike back was Banjuwangi, a town at the eastern tip of Java whence departs the ferry across the Bali Strait to the Indonesian island of Bali. There, a few days after the coup attempt in Djakarta, the Communists launched a full-scale attack on Ansor members. They were not armed with sophisticated weapons. According to Ansor, the Communists came at them wielding swords, knives, and sharpened stakes, but they killed 61 Ansor youths. Their leader, according to Ansor members, was an army surgeon. (This story does coincide with reports that the army medical corps was particularly effectively infiltrated by the Communist Party.) Though the army and Ansor later took control of the town, Communist subversion continued for some time.

Kediri, the Site of the Worst of It

East Java's worst slaughter took place in the Kediri district, where the military commander was a brother of General Sutojo, one of the six top generals murdered in Djakarta. Here thousands of Communist Party members were killed, mainly by Ansor squads, in a kind of holy war that had the blessing of the local Moslem leader, Hadji Makrus Ali. Explaining the killings as the "will of God," he said that the Communists got no more than they deserved.

The district is conveniently close to the Brantas River, and it was into this that the slashed bodies of the Communists were tumbled.

To keep the bodies from floating into irrigation channels leading off the river, the executioners protected the mouths of the channels with crude bamboo gates that let the water through, but deflected the corpses.

The killing in East Java was to leave a particularly bitter legacy. From this area were recruited many members of the Indonesian Marine Corps and Air Force. Many lost members of their families in the anti-Communist purge. It was a grudge they would not easily forget.

An Indonesian Émigré Describes the Tensions Around Communism in 1965 and After

Pipit Rochijat

*Pipit Rochijat is an Indonesian émigré and intellectual. In the fol-
lowing viewpoint, he discusses his refusal to identify as PKI or
non-PKI, suggesting that, in Indonesia, the designation is similar
to an ethnic identity. To illustrate the difficulties of the term, he
tells the story of M. Kartawidjaja, an anti-Communist sugar factory manager who, nonetheless, sheltered many Communists during the 1965 purges.*

The questions "PKI or Non-PKI," and "Marxist or Non-
Marxist" are exactly the same as the questions "Chinese or
Non-Chinese," "Chinese Halfbreed or Non-Chinese Halfbreed,"
"Arab or Non-Arab," "Muslim-extremist or Non-Muslimextremist," and so forth. Questions in this vein do not raise the
issue of a person's views or thought, merely that of his or her
"color." If the "color" isn't desirable, then neither are the views.
But all this aside, I refuse to answer questions of this type. My
reasons I append below. Let me ask forgiveness in advance if they
seem too long. It can't be helped.

Pipit Rochijat, "Am I PKI or Non-PKI?," trans. Benedict Anderson, *Indonesia*, no. 40,
October 1985. Copyright © 1985 by Southeast Asia Program Publications. All rights reserved. Reproduced by permission.

The PKI vs. Kartawidjaja

After his transfer in 1959 from the Semboro sugar factory in Jember, M. Kartawidjaja held the post of director of the Ngadirejo sugar factory in Kediri up until 1967. In 1967–68 he became Inspector of Sugar Factories in Semarang. In the following year he was appointed Director-in-Chief of State Plantation XXI in Situbondo, and took up his quarters in Surabaya. . . .

Twenty-five kilometers east of Kediri lay the debris of the former Jengkol sugar factory. In the old days, it had been a privately owned sugar factory, but then it was destroyed in the war [i.e., Revolution of 1945–49]. What survived was only the houses of the employees and the vast, scattered lands of the plantation itself. In 1962 the Department of Agriculture planned to unify these various sugar lands in the Jengkol area and then integrate them with the Ngadirejo sugar factory. In this way the sugar acreage owned by the Ngadirejo sugar factory would be greatly enlarged and its productive capacity greatly increased. Unfortunately, this plan for unifying the plantation land-holdings meant sacrificing the homes of local residents. These people would have to move out, and be relocated in places designated/set aside by the government. Now this plan was opposed by the PKI along with its mass organizations, such as the Barisan Tani Indonesia (BTI [Indonesian Peasant League]), the Gerakan Wanita Indonesia (Gerwani [Indonesian Women's Movement]), the SBG, or the Pemuda Rakyat [People's Youth]. When their protests had no effect, in the end the masses assembled within the PKI could no longer be controlled. They buried alive a bulldozer driver and a policeman. This aksi [demonstration] aroused a reaction in turn. Troops were brought in, and the PKI masses resisted them. The story goes that those in the front line were members of Gerwani. Maybe people thought that no way would the troops fire on women. But in the end, the soldiers did fire. And PKI victims fell. In fact so many victims fell that the news was reported in Radio Australia's Indonesian language broadcasts. And this clash proved to be the beginning of the conflict between the PKI (especially the SBG) and M. Kartawidjaja.

From that time on, at every opportunity—whether rallies or parades/processions—these slogans always appeared: "Retool Karta," "Karta Kabir," "Karta ex-Masyumi," "Karta Seven Village Devils," and so on—all terms currently popular at that time.

And Kartawidjaja's five sons were constantly forced to listen to abuse and read the slogans displayed in their [the PKI's] banners. Their ears got pretty red, their hearts felt on fire, and their thirst for revenge steadily increased.

Aside from rallies and parades, the SBG also continually organized demonstrations at the sugar factory. In addition to "Retool Karta," etc., their demands included "provision of buses for the children of workers who want to go to school in Kediri.". . .

In the period just prior to G30S [the September 30th coup], Kartawidjaja's policy in dealing with the SBG's demands became ever more disliked. For example, he dealt with strikes by workers who joined and were organized by the SBG by cutting their wages. And then gave the money as bonuses to those workers who did not strike. . . .

The Situation During G30S 1965

Up to 1965, the [national] front was divided in two: on the one side the Communist Front, and on the other the United Nationalist-Religious Front. And their respective strengths were about evenly balanced. . . .

The events of October 1, 1965 are something difficult, impossible to forget. The atmosphere was so tense, as though everyone was expecting something [catastrophic] once the takeover of power in Jakarta had been broadcast. All Kartawidjaja said to his family was: "Watch out, be very careful. Something's gone very wrong in Jakarta." Usually the doors and windows of the house were shut around 10:00 P.M., but on October 1 they were closed at 7:00. Fear seized the Kartawidjaja family, for the rumor that the PKI had made a coup and murdered the generals was already spreading. The PKI's own aggressive attitude and the way in which the generals had been killed strengthened the suspicion of PKI involvement. "Such brutal murders could only be the work of kafirs, i.e., the Communists," was the kind of comment that one then heard. At the same time, the Kartawidjaja family felt very thankful that General Nasution had escaped with his life. The only pity was that his little daughter was beyond rescue. For almost two weeks, everything was quiet in the Kediri region. People merely stayed on the alert and tensely watchful. In State High School No. 1 too the atmosphere was very heated. Reports that it was the PKI that had gone into rebellion spread rapidly. . . .

About two weeks after the events of October 1, the NU [a Muslim group] (especially their Ansor Youth) began to move, holding demonstrations. . . . They demanded the dissolution of the PKI, and that the death of each general be paid for with those of 100,000 Communists. Offices and other buildings owned by the PKI were attacked and reduced to rubble by the demonstrators. It was said that about 11 Communists died for nothing, simply because they were foolish enough to feel bound to defend PKI property. In an atmosphere of crisis suffused with so much hatred for the PKI, everything became permissible. After all, wasn't it everyone's responsibility to fight the kafir? And vengeance against the PKI seemed only right, since people felt that the Party had gone beyond the pale. So, the fact that only 11 Communists had [so far] died was regarded as completely inadequate. This kind of thinking also infected Kartawidjaja's Son No. 2.

Wanted: Communists

Once the mesmerizing calm had ended, the massacres began. Not only the NU masses, but also those of the PNI joined in. The army didn't get much involved. First to be raided were workers' quarters at the sugar factory. Usually at night . . . to eliminate the Communist elements. It was done like this: a particular village would be surrounded by squads of Nationalist and Religious

Youth (Muslim and Christian [Protestant], for example in Pare). A mass of Ansor Youth would be brought in. . . . On average, about 3,000 people would be involved. The expectation was that, with the village surrounded, no Communist elements would be able to escape.

It was pretty effective too. Each day, as Kartawidjaja's Son No. 2 went to, or returned from, State Senior High School No. 1, he always saw corpses of Communists floating in the River Brantas. The thing was that the school was located to the "kulon" (west) of the river. And usually the corpses were no longer recognizable as human. Headless. Stomachs torn open. The smell was unbelievable. To make sure they didn't sink, the carcasses were deliberately tied to, or impaled on, bamboo stakes. And the departure of corpses from the Kediri region down the Brantas achieved its golden age when bodies were stacked together on rafts over which the PKI banner proudly flew. . . .

Naturally, such mass killings were welcomed by the Nationalist and Religious groups. Indeed, [they felt,] the target of 100,000 Communist lives for 1 general's had to be achieved. It was the same for Kartawidjaja's Son No. 2 and his family. Especially when they got the word that for the Kartawidjaja family a Crocodile Hole[1] had been prepared, for use if the PKI were victorious.

This atmosphere of vengeance spread everywhere. Not merely in the outside world, but even into the schools, for example State High School No. 1. There the atmosphere was all the more ripe in that for all practical purposes the school broke down, and classes did not continue as usual. Many students did not come to school at all, like Syom, for example, a friend of Kartawidjaja's Son No. 2, who had to spend most of his time going round helping purge the Kediri region of Communist elements. Kartawidjaja's Son No. 2 saw many cases where teachers and student members of IPPI [League of Indonesian High School Students] at State High School No. 1 were held up at knife point by their Nationalist and Religious comrades. With the knives at their throats they were threatened with death. They wept, begging forgiveness and expressing regret for what they had done while members of IPPI. In the end all the secrets came out (or maybe false confessions). Each person tried to save himself at another's expense. After all, they were human beings too, and thus still wished to enjoy life.

Saving the Communists

Next: even though Kartawidjaja was hated by the PKI, on one occasion he told Kartawidjaja's Son No. 2 to go to the home of pak Haryo, an employee who lived next door and was an activist in the SBG. Kartawidjaja told him to fetch pak Haryo to the house and have him sleep there, bringing with him whatever clothes he needed. But since it was then pretty late at night, when Kartawidjaja's Son No. 2 knocked at the door, pak Haryo's family made no response. Maybe they were afraid that it might be the Angel of Death come visiting. The next morning, Kartawidjaja came himself to pick up pak Haryo. Subsequently he was taken by Kartawidjaja to Surabaya, to be hidden there.

Naturally, helping Communists wasn't at all in line with the ideas of Kartawidjaja's Son No. 2. So he asked: "Dad, why are you of all people protecting pak Haryo?" "Pak Haryo doesn't know a thing, and besides it would be a shame with all his kids."

Kartawidjaja was fortunate in that he was always informed about "who and who" was to lose his life. And many Communists who had once vilified Kartawidjaja now came to his house to ask for protection. On one occasion he set aside a special space in the meeting hall where people asking for his protection could overnight.

All through the purges, the mosques were packed with Communist visitors. Even the Workers' Hall was specially made over into a place for Friday prayers. As a result, many people judged that the PKI people had now become *sadar* [aware: of their past errors, of Allah's truth]. And hopes for survival became increasingly widespread. And at one of these Friday prayers, Kartawidjaja was asked to make a speech in front of all the assembled worshippers. He told them that "praying isn't compulsory. Don't force people to do it. Let those who want to pray pray. And if people don't want to, then they don't have to."

The interesting thing is that even though Kartawidjaja spoke in this vein (just imagine, in a time like that, the slightest thing could get one accused of being a Communist), and even though he protected many PKI people, he was never accused of being a Communist or involved in G30S. In fact, with the triumph of the Nationalist and Religious groups over the Communists, Kartawidjaja was appointed as adviser to the East Java Sarbumusi and the East Java KBG. And many of his friends—especially Islamic leaders (even till today)—came to his house. . . .

PKI or Non-PKI Is Not Important

With this brief background sketch now provided (a full account is still in process), I am ready to answer the question: am I PKI or not? As a matter of principle, I refuse to answer questions of this type. For in essence they are the same kind of questions as: "You're a Chinese, aren't you?" "You're a Chinese halfbreed, aren't you?" "You're an Arab, aren't you?" And so on. If you're a Communist, then your opinions are [automatically] no good. If you're a Chinese, then (all the more so!) your intentions are no good. Questions of this kind serve only to show that in the mind of the questioner what is important is not really opinions, but simply "color." Aside from whether he was a Communist or not, Mao [the Communist leader of China] managed to feed the immense population of the PRC [People's Republic of China]. Aside from whether he is a Muslim or not, [Colonel Muammar] Gaddafi [head of Libya] has managed to create a society worthy of imitation. So what's the point of claiming that we are more Pancasilaist [that is, closer to Indonesian ideals] than anyone, when on the one hand the common people [rakyat] live on the edge of starvation, and on the other the powers-that-be live it up. As my father used to say, "You can even be a Communist if you want to"—though he didn't like the idea—"so long as you have principles." And I feel the same way. People can call you whatever they like—that's up to them to evaluate/judge. And I certainly wouldn't try to forbid them from doing so. If you want to do something you regard as right, well that's up to you. If you choose to have the mentality of the Chinese businessmen when my father still held office (i.e., if need be, put on a smiling face), that's OK. If you want to butter up the Communists so as to get certain amenities of life, but then pretend to forget this when the atmosphere changes and people start ridiculing "PKI hangers-on," that's OK too. If you choose to outyell everyone else with your "revolutionary" demands as a way of winning friends in certain quarters, and then feel compelled to put all gears in reverse in order to survive, well that's OK too. If you want to be two-faced, claiming to be a leftist in front of leftists, and a true loyalist in the presence of the powers-that-be, that too is all right.

For all these reasons, comrades [of] mine (watch out though if you use this terminology, since, so far as I know, the only person who liked to use it was Aidit, the king of Indonesian Communists in the old days; before you know it, you could be accused of being a Communist!): don't keep on asking what I am. I myself never give a damn where you come from and what your color is. "It's up to you, take care of it yourself. The important thing is simply to have some principles."

Now to conclude. The truth is that I have the following fantasy: How wonderful it would be if the Communists were totally wiped out, so that the world would be permanently rid of communism. Then the question "Are you Communist or non-Communist?" would become unimaginable. Next, all the Muslim extremists would be cut down to the last man. Then the question "Are you a Muslimextremist or a Non-Muslimextremist?" would never arise. And if need be, non-Muslimextremists could also be eliminated. After that, the Chinese would be eradicated root and branch. Then the question "Are you a Chinese or a non-Chinese?" wouldn't exist. To put it in a nutshell, everything regarded as filthy would be wiped clean. And once the world was completely clean, only one simple question would remain: "You [*sic*, in English], you're re . . . lated to Pak Harto, aren't you?" Now then . . . what would happen next?

Note:

1. Lubang Buaya (Crocodile Hole) was the name for the area . . . where the bodies of the assassinated generals were disposed of (down a disused well). In 1965–66 a successful psychological warfare campaign was launched by the army to persuade anti-Communist notables and political leaders that the PKI had secretly prepared thousands of comparable "holes" for their burial after execution.

Indonesians Recount Their Role in the 1965 Massacres

Anthony Deutsch

Anthony Deutsch is a journalist who has worked for Reuters, the Financial Times, *and the Associated Press. In the following viewpoint, he relates the accounts of four Indonesian Muslims who participated in the massacre of Communists in 1965. In their accounts, the killers express no regret and explain that they were fighting to protect their religion and keep Indonesia free of Communists. Deutsch also interviews human rights workers who say that Indonesia must confront its past and provide justice to those who were murdered.*

The men bound the thumbs of dozens of suspected communists behind their backs with banana leaves and drove them to a torch-lit jungle clearing. As villagers jeered, the prisoners were killed, one by one.

Four Discuss the Killings

"There was no resistance," remembers Sulchan, then the 21-year-old deputy commander of an Islamic youth militia. "All of them had their throats cut with a long sword."

Sulchan was a killer in one of the worst atrocities of the 20th century, where up to half a million people were massacred in 1965–66 in a purge of communists backed by the United States government. The bloodbath swept into power the dictator Suharto, who ruled for three decades. Today, Indonesian history books make no mention of any deaths, and government and military officials depict what happened as a necessary national uprising against a communist threat.

In a series of interviews with The Associated Press, Sulchan and three other killers said the massacres were in fact a carefully planned and executed state operation and described some of its horrors for the first time. In their rare testimony, all the men spoke of what they did with detachment and often pride, and expressed no regret at what they described as defending their country and religion, Islam.

The CIA refuses to talk about the operation even today, citing security reasons. But documents released by the National Security Archives in Washington, D.C., show that the U.S. Embassy passed the names of dozens of Communist Party leaders, and possibly many more, to the Indonesian army, along with some of their locations. Documents also show that officials from the U.S. Embassy in Indonesia passed on information to Washington about the killings of 50 to 100 people every night.

The U.S. Embassy declined to comment.

Even after Suharto's death in January [2008], many who aided the purge are still in positions of power or influence, including former and current government, military and intelligence leaders, experts say. And the suppression of information about the abuses of the era means there has been no meaningful redress for the families of the dead.

"In all the newspapers and magazines published since late 1965, it is extraordinarily rare to find a perpetrator's description of the killings," says John Roosa, a professor at the University of British Columbia who wrote the book *Pretext for Mass Murder*.

Sulchan, an Indonesian Muslim cleric, stands in front of his mosque in Bangil, Indonesia, in 2008. He has revealed his involvement in the atrocities that occurred against the Communists. © Trisnadi/AP Photo.

Eliminate All Communists

The testimony of the four men gives a glimpse into how the killings unfolded.

The frenzy began shortly after Sept. 30, 1965, after an apparent abortive coup in which six right-wing generals were murdered and dumped in a well near the capital, Jakarta. Suharto, an unknown major general at the time, stepped into the power vacuum. He blamed the assassinations on Indonesia's Communist Party and claimed they were targeting Islamic leaders.

No conclusive proof of communist involvement in the coup has been produced, but the party was then the largest outside the Soviet Union and China, with some 3 million members. It also had an armed wing and serious financial clout. Its growing ties with China and Russia worried Washington, at a time when the Vietnam War was intensifying and fears of communist takeovers in Southeast Asia were running high.

The four men interviewed by the AP were members of the local Islamic youth militia, Banser, or of anti-communist youth movements in East Java. They were in their 20s at the time, and Sulchan and his superior jointly commanded a 200-member branch of Banser.

Sulchan, now a 64-year-old preacher, says the "order to eliminate all communists" came through Islamic clerics with Indonesia's largest Muslim organization, Nahdlatul Ulama. Sulchan led the first killing in his neighborhood—that of a schoolteacher, Hamid, said to have had communist ties.

We "hit him in the head with a sledgehammer and he died instantly," says Sulchan, a tall, lanky man who wears a wraparound Javanese sarong, his crooked teeth stained by years of smoking sweet clove cigarettes. He points calmly up the street to the spot of the murder, a piece of cracked pavement and an abandoned kiosk overgrown with weeds.

On another day, his men decapitated a man named Darmo because they feared he would return to life and take revenge. His head was hung from a banyan tree in the town square and his body dumped on the other side of the river, says Sulchan, sitting on the tiled floor of his mosque.

On one night, Sulchan's platoon helped unload 20 to 30 prisoners at the execution site and beat to death a man who tried to escape. The rest were forced to the ground and killed. A man pleaded with his executor to tell his child to study the Quran, Islam's holy book. The executor agreed, then murdered him too.

The bodies were dumped in a ditch. Such scenes were repeated across Java, Sumatra and the eastern island of Bali for several months in 1965 and 1966.

I Felt Righteous

"I am convinced the actions were justified because communists were the enemy of my religion," says Sulchan. "I thought: This is what people get for not submitting to religion. I felt righteous."

Sulchan's superior, Mansur, commanded the Banser militia for two years and describes a highly efficient operation. Mansur, who like many Indonesians goes by one name only, collected the names of suspected communists in the region. Their houses were marked in red on maps, and he ordered his men to round them up.

Those who resisted were killed on the spot. Others were taken to detention centers, then trucked to killing fields and shot, stabbed, beheaded and beaten to death, he says. He saw the slaying of hundreds of unarmed detainees in his village, whose remains now lie beneath an unmarked, trash-strewn lot.

"We didn't want the country to become a communist state," says Mansur, sitting on a porch bench after returning from Friday afternoon prayers, wearing a tidy Indonesian batik shirt, thin spectacles and an Islamic cap. "I don't have any regrets."

A few miles away, businesses and homes said to be communist were plundered and their owners driven away, says Munib Habib, who led an anti-communist student movement. The houses belonged to Indonesian-Chinese, a much-resented minority in Indonesia targeted again in 1998 riots that left hundreds dead.

"We were informed by a spy that they were hoarding staple foods. We went to the shops and dragged out the owners," says Habib, now a 64-year-old Muslim cleric and local politician.

Satuman, a former member of the youth wing of the National Party who now lives in a simple cement house with his son, says the kidnappings and killings targeted not only known communists, but retired army and navy members, peasants and teachers.

He says he saw people taken in trucks from the local prison for mass killings in the evening. About 60 people were shoved to the ground and butchered as they screamed, he says. Then the bodies were dumped in a freshly dug trench, some of the victims apparently still alive.

"The soldiers opened fire into the hole," remembers Satuman, 68.

The men spoke proudly of saving the nation from a communist takeover targeting Islamic leaders. However, the claim that the massacres were necessary is baseless, Roosa says.

"Most of the killings were simple executions of helpless detainees," he says.

Justice Still Needed

Even today, a ban on the Communist Party remains in force in Indonesia, and people marked as ex-political prisoners endure lingering mistrust and discrimination. Witnesses to the state-sponsored killings were silenced under the Suharto dictatorship, fearing kidnapping, imprisonment or even death.

Suharto commanded widespread respect, with the Indonesian president and tens of thousands of mourners attending his funeral in January [2008]. But shortly after, Indonesia's Human Rights Commission launched an inquiry into the abuses of his reign. And the New York-based Human Rights Watch believes the perpetrators should be put on trial to "open up an important chapter of Indonesia's history that remains all but taboo more than 40 years after the fact.

"Justice, accountability, and an end to impunity are not just about the past," says Brad Adams, who heads the group's Asian division.

Gustaf Dupe, who says he spent four years in jail without trial and was tortured and beaten, leads an association of 6,500 family members pushing for the government to acknowledge its role in the killings and return confiscated property.

"Some mass graves have been discovered," says Dupe. "But there is still opposition to digging them up, identifying the bodies and reburying them in a humane and religious way."

Glossary

Ansor The youth wing of the Nahdlatul Ulama, the largest Islamic organization in Indonesia. In 1965, Ansor members were recruited in large numbers to serve in anti-Communist militias.

Bali A province of Indonesia, covering the island of Bali and a few small neighboring islands. The island is home to most of Indonesia's Hindus.

East Timor The eastern half of the island of Timor, and a few nearby islands. It was a Portuguese colony occupied by Indonesia in 1975. It gained independence in 2002.

Guided Democracy President Sukarno's term for an autocracy with democratic elements. Elections are held to legitimize the government but have little power to change it. The term has been used in other countries, including Russia.

Java An Indonesian island—and the world's most populist island. It is politically, culturally, and economically central to Indonesia.

Nasakom A political concept introduced by President Sukarno based on the Indonesian words nasionalisme (nationalism), agama (religion), and kommunisme (communism).

New Order The term used to refer to President Suharto's reign (1965–1998).

NU Nahdlatul Ulama, the largest Islamic organization in Indonesia.

Pancasila The official philosophical foundation of the Indonesian state. It includes the principles of belief in God, civilization, unity, democracy, and justice.

PKI The Indonesian Communist Party.

Suharto A military officer who took power in Indonesia in 1965 and ruled until 1998.

Sukarno The leader of Indonesia's struggle for independence from the Netherlands, and the first president of Indonesia.

Organizations to Contact

The editors have compiled the following list of organizations concerned with the issues debated in this book. The descriptions are derived from materials provided by the organizations. All have publications or information available for interested readers. The list was compiled on the date of publication of the present volume; the information provided here may change. Be aware that many organizations take several weeks or longer to respond to inquiries, so allow as much time as possible.

Amnesty International
5 Penn Plaza, 14th Floor
New York, NY 10001
(212) 807-8400 • fax: (212) 463-9193
e-mail: aimember@aiusa.org
website: www.amnestyusa.org

Amnesty International is a worldwide movement of people who campaign for internationally recognized human rights. Its vision is of a world in which every person enjoys all of the human rights enshrined in the Universal Declaration of Human Rights and other international human rights standards. Each year it publishes a report on its work and its concerns throughout the world.

East Timor and Indonesia Action Network (ETAN)
PO Box 21873
Brooklyn, NY 11202-1873
(718) 596-7668
e-mail: etan@etan.org
website: www.etan.org

ETAN was founded to support self-determination and human rights for the people of East Timor. It lobbies to change US foreign policy and to raise publicity for the cause of independence for East Timor. Its website includes numerous reports and articles on human rights, East Timor, and Indonesia.

Embassy of the Republic of Indonesia
2020 Massachusetts Avenue NW
Washington, DC 20036
(202) 775-5300 • fax: (202) 775-5365
website: www.embassyofindonesia.org

The Embassy of the Republic of Indonesia is the official diplomatic embassy of Indonesia in the United States. Its website includes information and articles on Indonesia, on US/Indonesian relations, on Indonesian's foreign policy, news and press releases.

Human Rights First
333 Seventh Avenue, 13th Floor
New York, NY 10001-5108
(202) 845-5200 • fax: (212) 845-5399
e-mail: feedback@humanrightsfirst.org
website: www.humanrightsfirst.org

Human Rights First is an independent advocacy and action organization that presses the US government and private companies to respect human rights and the rule of law. It also develops policy solutions to support human rights. Its website includes press releases, news, and reports on human rights issues around the globe.

Human Rights Watch
350 Fifth Avenue, 34th Floor
New York, NY 10118-3299
(212) 290-4700 • fax: (212) 736-1300
e-mail: hrwnyc@hrw.org
website: www.hrw.org

Founded in 1978, this nongovernmental organization conducts systematic investigations of human rights abuses in countries around the world. It publishes many books and reports on specific countries and issues as well as annual reports and other articles. Its website includes numerous discussions of human rights and international justice issues.

International Center for Transitional Justice (ICTJ)
5 Hanover Square, Floor 24
New York, NY 10004
(917) 637-3800
e-mail: info@ictj.com
website: http://ictj.org

ICTJ works to help societies in transition address the legacy of human rights violations. Working with international organizations, governments, victims' groups, and activists, it provides technical expertise and knowledge of relevant comparable experiences in transitional justice. It also researches, analyzes, and reports on transitional justice developments worldwide. ICTJ has worked in Indonesia to help address the human rights violations of the Suharto era, and its website includes reports and news updates on human rights issues in Indonesia.

Montreal Institute for Genocide and Human Rights Studies (MIGS)
Concordia University
1455 De Maisonneuve Boulevard West
Montreal, Quebec H3G 1M8
Canada
(514) 848-2424, ext. 5729 or 2404 • fax: (514) 848-4538
website: http://migs.concordia.ca

MIGS, founded in 1986, monitors native-language media for early warning signs of genocide in countries deemed to be at risk of mass atrocities. The institute houses the Will to Intervene (W2I) Project, a research initiative focused on the prevention of genocide and other mass atrocity crimes. The institute also collects and disseminates research on the historical origins of mass killings and provides comprehensive links to this and other research materials on its website. Additionally, the website provides numerous links to other websites focused on genocide and related issues, as well as specialized sites organized by nation, region, or case.

STAND/United to End Genocide
1025 Connecticut Avenue, Suite 310
Washington, DC 20036
(202) 556-2100
e-mail: info@standnow.org
website: www.standnow.org

STAND is the student-led division of United to End Genocide (formerly Genocide Intervention Network). STAND envisions a world in which the global community is willing and able to protect civilians from genocide and mass atrocities. In order to empower individuals and communities with the tools to prevent and stop genocide, STAND recommends activities—from engaging government representatives to hosting fund-raisers— and has more than one thousand student chapters at colleges and high schools. While maintaining many documents online regarding genocide, STAND provides a plan to promote action as well as education.

TAPOL
111 Northwood Road
Thornton Heath, Surrey CR7 8HW
UK
44 020 8771 2904 • fax: 44 020 8653 0322
e-mail: tapol@gn.apc.org
website: www.gn.apc.org/tapol

TAPOL campaigns for human rights, peace, and democracy in Indonesia. It works to raise awareness of human rights issues in Indonesia, including in West Papua, and works closely with local organizations in Indonesia. Its website includes news releases and reports.

United Human Rights Council (UHRC)
104 N. Belmont Street, Suite 313
Glendale, CA 91206
(818) 507-1933
website: www.unitedhumanrights.org

UHRC is a committee of the Armenian Youth Federation. By means of action on a grass-roots level, the UHRC works toward exposing and correcting human rights violations of governments worldwide. The UHRC campaigns against violators in an effort to generate awareness through boycotts, community outreach, and education. The UHRC website focuses on the genocides of the twentieth century.

List of Primary Source Documents

The editors have compiled the following list of documents that either broadly address genocide and persecution or more narrowly focus on the topic of this volume. The full text of these documents is available from multiple sources in print and online.

Convention Against Torture and Other Cruel, Inhuman, or Degrading Punishment, United Nations, 1974

A draft resolution adopted by the United Nations General Assembly in 1974 opposing any nation's use of torture, unusually harsh punishment, and unfair imprisonment.

Convention on the Prevention and Punishment of the Crime of Genocide, December 9, 1948

A resolution of the United Nations General Assembly that defines genocide in legal terms and advises participating countries to prevent and punish actions of genocide in war and peacetime.

Principles of International Law Recognized in the Charter of the Nuremburg Tribunal, United Nations International Law Commission, 1950

After World War II (1939–1945), the victorious allies legally tried surviving leaders of Nazi Germany in the German city of Nuremburg. The proceedings established standards for international law that were affirmed by the United Nations and by later court tests. Among other standards, national leaders can be held responsible for crimes against humanity, which might include "murder, extermination, deportation, enslavement, and other inhuman acts."

Rome Statute of the International Criminal Court, July 17, 1998

The treaty that established the International Criminal Court. It establishes the court's functions, jurisdiction, and structure.

Statement of the Delegation of the Central Committee of the Communist Party of Indonesia in Commemoration of the 48th Anniversary of the Founding of the Party, May 23, 1968

A publication by the PKI, or Indonesian Communist Party, analyzing the 1965 attacks on them and restating their opposition to the government and their commitment to workers.

Suharto's Resignation Speech, May 21, 1998

Suharto, the longtime ruler of Indonesia who gained power following the 1965 killings in Indonesia, announces his resignation after widespread popular uprisings and unrest.

Sukarno's Speech to the Asian African Conference, Bandung, Indonesia, April 18, 1955

President Sukarno of Indonesia discusses his hopes for the rising nations in Asia and Africa and his concerns about the continuing legacy of colonialism.

United Nations General Assembly Resolution 96 on the Crime of Genocide, December 11, 1946

A resolution of the United Nations General Assembly that affirms that genocide is a crime under international law.

Universal Declaration of Human Rights, United Nations, 1948

Soon after its founding, the United Nations approved this general statement of individual rights it hoped would apply to citizens of all nations.

Whitaker Report on Genocide, 1985

This report addresses the question of the prevention and punishment of the crime of genocide. It calls for the establishment of an international criminal court and a system of universal jurisdiction to ensure that genocide is punished.

For Further Research

Books

Benedict R. Anderson, *Violence and the State in Suharto's Indonesia*. Ithaca, NY: Southeast Asia Program, 2000.

R.E. Elson, *Suharto: A Political Biography*. Cambridge, UK: Cambridge University Press, 2002.

Tineke Hellwig, *The Indonesia Reader: History, Culture, Politics*. Durham, NC: Duke University Press, 2009.

Max Lane, *Catastrophe in Indonesia*. New York: Seagull, 2010.

Max Lane, *Unfinished Nation: Indonesia Before and After Suharto*. New York: Verso, 2008.

Rachmi Diyah Larasati, *The Dance That Makes You Vanish: Cultural Reconstruction in Post-Genocide Indonesia*. Minneapolis: University of Minnesota Press, 2013.

Richard Lloyd Parry, *In the Time of Madness: Indonesia on the Edge of Chaos*. New York: Random House, 2005.

John Roosa, *Pretext for Mass Murder: The September 30th Movement and Suharto's Coup d'État in Indonesia*. Madison: University of Wisconsin-Madison, 2006.

Adrian Vickers, *A History of Modern Indonesia, Second Edition*. Cambridge, UK: Cambridge University Press, 2013.

André Vltchek, *Indonesia: Archipelago of Fear*. London: Pluto, 2012.

Periodicals and Internet Sources

Benedict Anderson, "From Miracle to Crash," *London Review of Books*, vol. 20, no. 8, April 16, 1998. www.lrb.co.uk.

Eric Bellman, "Sentences in Indonesian Killings Draw Criticism," *Wall Street Journal*, July 28, 2011. http://online.wsj.com.

Marilyn Berger, "Suharto Dies at 86; Indonesian Dictator Brought Order and Bloodshed," *New York Times*, January 28, 2008. www.nytimes.com.

John Braddock, "Historian Says US Backed 'Efficacious Terror' in 1965 Indonesian Massacre," World Socialist Web Site, July 7, 2009. www.wsws.org.

"CIA Stalling State Department Histories," George Washington University's National Security Archive, July 27, 2001. www.gwu.edu.

Robert Cribb, "Unresolved Problems in the Indonesian Killings of 1965–1966," *Asian Survey*, vol. 42, no. 4, July–August 2002, pp. 560–563.

Anthony Deutsch, "Mass Killings Under Suharto Recalled," *Boston Globe*, January 28, 2008. www.boston.com.

John Gittings, "Obituary: Suharto," *Guardian*, January 27, 2008. www.guardian.co.uk.

Conn Hallinan, "*New York Times* Continues to Conceal U.S. Role in 1965 Indonesia Coup," Foreign Policy in Focus, January 23, 2012. www.fpif.org.

Ulma Haryanto, "Former Sukarno Palace Dancer Still Battling PKI Ghosts," *Jakarta Globe*, March 8, 2012. www.thejakartaglobe.com.

Edward S. Herman, "Good and Bad Genocide: Double Standards in Coverage of Suharto and Pol Pot," Third World Traveler, September–October 1998. www.thirdworldtraveler.com.

John Hughes, "Report on Indonesia," *Atlantic*, December 1967. www.theatlantic.com.

Ron Jenkins, "'The Act of Killing'—Documenting Delusion," *Jakarta Post*, October 18, 2012. www.thejakartapost.com.

Robert Manne, "Apologetics and Hypocrisy: An Exchange on Australian Anticommunism and the Indonesian Massacre of 1965-6 Between Gerard Henderson and Robert Manne," *The Monthly*, September 2008. www.themonthly.com.

Nathaniel Mehr, "Remembering the Indonesian Killings," *London Progressive Journal*, June 5, 2009. http://london progressivejournal.com.

Sara Schonhardt, "Veil of Silence Lifted in Indonesia," *New York Times*, January 18, 2012. www.nytimes.com.

Ezra Sihite, "Little Government Remorse Evident Over Indonesia's 1965 Killings," *Jakarta Globe*, October 2, 2012. www.thejakartaglobe.com.

Grace Susetyo, "Documentary: The 1965–66 Purge of Alleged Communists in Indonesia Left One Million Dead," *Constantine Report*, January 4, 2013. www.constantine report.com.

Kai Thaler, "Foreshadowing Future Slaughter: From the Indonesian Killings of 1965–1966 to the 1974–1999 Genocide in East Timor," *Genocide Studies and Prevention*, vol. 7, no. 2/3, August 2012. http://utpjournals.metapress.com.

Abigail Abrash Walton, "Indonesia After Suharto," Foreign Policy in Focus, November 1, 1998. www.fpif.org.

Websites and Films

40 Years of Silence: An Indonesian Tragedy (2009) Directed by Robert Lemelson, Elemental Productions. Anthropologist Robert Lemelson focuses on the testimonies of four individuals from Central Java and Bali who were affected by the 1965 mass killings in Indonesia.

The Living Memory Project (http://sea.lib.niu.edu) A web project archiving photographs and videos related to the atrocities by Indonesia in East Timor in the early 1990s.

The Sukarno Years: Birth of the Republic of Indonesia (www
.sukarnoyears.com) A website devoted to Indonesia during
the rule of Sukarno from 1945 to 1967. It includes articles
on domestic policy and foreign policy, and an extensive section on the political background of the 1965–1966 violence.

Index